EVERYTHING ABOUT MR. LEMONCELLO'S IMAGINATION FACTORY WORLD HEADQUARTERS IN NEW YORK CITY WAS WILD AND WACKY.

There was a balloon store, a bookstore, and a bakery on the ground floor of the block-long building. The arched golden doorway into the Imagination Factory's lobby was guarded by a pair of mechanical bears in circus band uniforms blowing bubbles out of their trombones.

Once Kyle, Akimi, Angus, and Abia stepped into the lobby, they smelled cotton candy, popcorn, and caramel apples.

A man named Vader Nix, whose parents had been huge Star Wars fans, stepped out of a glass elevator (designed to look like a rocket ship) to greet them.

"Welcome to Lemoncello world headquarters," said Mr. Nix.

D0055095

MORE FAVORITES BY CHRIS GRABENSTEIN

MR. LEMONCELLO'S

GREAT LIBRARY
RACE

CHRIS GRABENSTEIN

A YEARLING BOOK

This is a work of fiction. Names, characters, places, and incidents either are the product of the author's imagination or are used fictitiously. Any resemblance to actual persons, living or dead, events, or locales is entirely coincidental.

Text copyright © 2017 by Chris Grabenstein
Cover art copyright © 2017 by Gilbert Ford

All rights reserved. Published in the United States by Yearling, an imprint of Random House Children's Books, a division of Penguin Random House LLC, New York. Originally published in hardcover in the United States by Random House Children's Books, New York, in 2017.

Yearling and the jumping horse design are registered trademarks of Penguin Random House LLC.

Visit us on the Web! rhcbooks.com

Educators and librarians, for a variety of teaching tools, visit us at RHTeachersLibrarians.com

The Library of Congress has cataloged the hardcover edition of this work as follows:
Names: Grabenstein, Chris, author.
Title: Mr. Lemoncello's great library race / Chris Grabenstein.
Description: First edition. | New York : Random House, [2017] | Sequel to: Mr. Lemoncello's Library Olympics. | Summary: "Mr. Lemoncello holds a contest for his young friends where they must bring interesting facts back to his library" —Provided by publisher.
Identifiers: LCCN 2015040525 | ISBN 978-0-553-53606-5 (trade) | ISBN 978-0-553-53607-2 (lib. bdg.) | ISBN 978-0-553-53608-9 (ebook)
Subjects: | CYAC: Libraries—Fiction. | Contests—Fiction. | Books and reading—Fiction. | Eccentrics and eccentricities—Fiction.
Classification: LCC PZ7.G7487 Mm 2016 | DDC [Fic]—dc23

ISBN 978-0-553-53609-6 (pbk.)

Printed in the United States of America
10 9 8 7 6 5 4 3 2 1
First Yearling Edition 2018

Random House Children's Books supports the First Amendment and celebrates the right to read.

For Barbara Bakowski and Alison Kolani
and all the other copyeditors
who have helped me keep my facts straight
even though I write fiction

This was a game Kyle Keeley refused to lose.

For the first time since Mr. Lemoncello's famous library escape contest, he was up against his old nemesis, Charles Chiltington.

"Surrender, Keeley!" Charles jeered from three spaces ahead. "Chiltingtons never lose!"

"Except, you know, when they do!" shouted Kyle's best friend, Akimi Hughes. She was ten spaces behind Kyle and couldn't stand seeing Charles in the lead.

The life-size board game had been rolled out like a plastic runner rug around the outer ring of tables in the Rotunda Reading Room of Mr. Lemoncello's library.

"The game's not over until it's over, Charles," Kyle said with a smile.

He had landed on a bright red question mark square, while Charles was safe on "Free Standing." A shaky collection of drifting holograms hovered over their heads, suspended in midair beneath the building's magnificent Wonder Dome. The dome's giant video screens were dark so they wouldn't interfere with the ghostly green images creating what Mr. Lemoncello called a Rube Goldberg contraption—a device deliberately designed to perform a very simple task in an extremely complicated way.

Most Rube Goldberg contraptions involve a chain reaction. In Mr. Lemoncello's Rickety-Trickety Fact or Fictiony game, a new piece of the chain was added every time one of the players gave an incorrect answer. If someone reached the finish line before all the pieces lined up, they won. However, if any player gave one too many wrong answers, they would trigger the chain reaction and end up trapped under a pointed dunce cap.

They would lose.

"Are you ready for your question, Mr. Keeley?" boomed Mr. Lemoncello, acting as the quiz master.

"Yes, sir," said Kyle.

"Fact or fiction for six," said Mr. Lemoncello, reading from a bright yellow game card. "At five feet four inches, George Washington was the shortest American president ever elected. Would you like to answer or do the research?"

It was a tough choice, especially since Kyle didn't know the answer.

If he did the research, he'd have to go back one space *and* lose a turn so he could look up the correct answer on one of the tablet computers built into the nearby reading desk.

But while he was researching, Charles might surge ahead. He might even make it all the way to the finish line.

On the other hand, even though Kyle didn't know the answer, if he said either "fact" *or* "fiction," he had a fifty-fifty chance of being right and moving forward six spaces, putting him *in front* of Charles, and that much closer to victory.

Of course, Kyle also had a fifty-fifty chance of being wrong and adding what might be the final hologram to the wobbly contraption overhead.

"Do the research, Kyle!" urged Akimi.

"Please do," sneered Charles.

"Yo!" shouted another one of Kyle's best buds, Miguel Fernandez. "Don't let Chiltington get under your dome, bro. He's just playing mind games with you."

"Impossible." Charles sniffed. "Keeley doesn't have a mind for me to play with."

"Uh, uh, uh," said Mr. Lemoncello. "Charles, I wonder if, just this once, you might choose kind?" He turned to Kyle. "Well, Mr. Keeley? No one can make this decision for you, unless, of course, you hire a professional decider, but trust me—they are decidedly expensive. Are you willing to put everything on a waffle and take a wild guess?"

Kyle hated losing a turn when the whole idea was to *win* the game. He hated going backward when the object was to move forward.

He studied the teetering collection of holograms suspended under the darkened dome. He looked at Charles, who was sneering back at him smugly.

"I want to answer, sir."

"Very well," said Mr. Lemoncello. "Let me repeat the question before the cucumbers I had for lunch repeat on me: At five feet four inches, George Washington was the shortest American president ever elected. Fact or fiction?"

Kyle took a deep breath. He remembered some teacher once saying people were shorter back in the olden days. So odds were that Washington was a shrimp.

"That, sir," he said, "is a . . . fact?"

A buzzer SCRONKed like a sick goose.

"Sorry," said Mr. Lemoncello. "It is, in fact, fiction. At six feet three inches, George Washington was one of our *tallest* presidents. It's time to add another piece to our dangling-dunce-cap-trap contraption."

Electronic notes diddled up a scale.

"Oh, dear," said Mr. Lemoncello. "It looks like that's the last straw!"

A hologram of a striped milk carton straw floated into place. It shot a spitball at a hologram of an old-fashioned cash register, which hit a button, which made the cash drawer pop open with a BING! The drawer smacked a holographic golf ball, which BOINKed down seven steps of a staircase one at a time until it bopped into a row of dominoes, which started to tumble in a curving line. The final domino triggered a catapult, which fired a

Ping-Pong ball, which smacked a rooster in the butt. The bird *cock-a-doodle-doo*ed, which startled a tiny man in a striped bathing suit standing on top of a fifty-foot ladder so much that he leapt off, spiraled down, and landed with a splash in a wooden bucket, which, since it was suddenly heavier, pulled a rope that struck a match, which lit a fuse, which ignited a fireworks rocket, which blasted off, which knocked the dunce cap off its hook.

The holographic hat of shame fell and covered Kyle like an upside-down ice cream cone.

"Loser!" crowed Charles.

Everybody else laughed.

By taking a wild guess, Kyle hadn't gone backward or lost a turn.

But he'd definitely lost the game!

Since the dunce cap was only a hologram, it couldn't actually trap Kyle.

But its laser-generated sides were equipped with motion sensors. So when Kyle tried to step out from under the flickering image of the giant parking-cone-shaped hat, he triggered some pretty embarrassing sound effects. Mostly gassy *BLATTs* and *FWUUUUUMPs*.

All the other players were cracking up, so Kyle took a goofy bow.

And activated the motion sensors again.

FWUUUUUMP!

"That's Keeley, all right," snickered Charles. "Nothing but windy blasts of gas."

"You're right," said Kyle, taking another bow and activating another *FWUUUUUMP!*

"And you were in the lead, Charles, so you win. Congratulations."

He stuck his hand in and out of the laser grid to blare a gassy fanfare to the tune of "Happy Birthday to You": *BLATT-BLATT-BLATT-BLATT, FWUMP-FWUMP!*

"All right," cried a no-nonsense voice in the midst of all the laughter. "Shut it down. Need to iron out that glitch."

There were six thumps and a loud whir, and then the holographic Rube Goldberg contraption disappeared. A bald man in a lab coat stepped out of the shadows, toting a tablet computer the size of a paperback.

"Switch on the Wonder Dome," he said to the flat screen he held in his palm.

Instantly, the ten wedge-shaped, high-definition video screens lining the library's colossal cathedral ceiling started shimmering as the dome went from black to its swirling, full-circle kaleidoscopic mode.

"Friends," announced Mr. Lemoncello, marching across the rotunda's marble floor toward the man in the white coat, "allow me to introduce you to the library's brand-new head imagineer, Mr. Chester 'Chet' Raymo, the genius behind my new Mind-Bogglingly Big 'n' Wacky Gymnasium Games!" He cleared his throat and warbled, *"Mr. Raymo is a brilliant brain-o! What he does is hard to explain-o!"*

Mr. Raymo was so busy tapping his tablet he didn't realize that Mr. Lemoncello was singing his praises.

The head imagineer wore thick black-rimmed glasses and a skinny black necktie and had seriously slumped shoulders. He looked like he could work at mission control for NASA.

"I believe we need to make a few minor adjustments before we roll it out to the schools," said Mr. Raymo. "Those sound effects activated when the loser attempted to escape were supposed to be burglar alarm bells, not farts."

"I know," said Mr. Lemoncello. "I changed them."

Mr. Raymo nodded. Tapped his tablet again.

"Duly noted."

"Thank you, Chet." Mr. Lemoncello threw open his arms and, in a very loud voice, addressed the players still standing in various spots along the game board.

"And thank you, one and all, for participating in this trial run of my newest gaming concept. Soon we will be able to take these same portable hologram projectors to gymnasiums, cafetoriums, and, if we hold our breath, natatoriums, so schools, even those with swimming pools, can use my life-size board games as fund-raisers—free of charge, of course."

"I really enjoyed the game," said Sierra Russell, Kyle's bookworm friend. "I was able to read two whole chapters while I waited for everybody else to spin and take their turns."

"It was awesome," agreed Kyle, who loved all of Mr. Lemoncello's wacky games, even the ones he lost.

"Totally!" added Miguel.

"It's a rip-off," scoffed Charles Chiltington, who'd been trying to run Mr. Lemoncello out of town ever since the eccentric billionaire first came home to Ohio and spent five hundred million dollars building Alexandriaville the most extraordinary high-tech library in the world.

"I beg your pardon, Charles?" said Mr. Lemoncello, blinking repeatedly. "A rip-off?"

"It's just a warmed-over version of that old parlor game Botticelli! You should be more inventive. Like the Krinkle brothers."

The Krinkle brothers owned a huge game company that, in Kyle's humble opinion, made extremely boring board games and dull generic stuff like Chinese checkers, pachisi, and dominoes. In fact, Kyle had come up with his own ad slogan for the rival game maker: "If it's a Krinkle, it's going to stinkle."

"See you later, losers." Charles marched out of the Rotunda Reading Room.

Kyle sometimes wondered why Charles was still allowed to come to the Lemoncello Library. He and his parents had done so much to try to wreck Mr. Lemoncello's dreams. Since Kyle (along with all the other "champions" from the recent Library Olympics) was now on the library's board of trustees, he once suggested that Charles (plus the rest of the Chiltington family) be banned from the building.

When he did, Mr. Lemoncello gasped, clutched his chest, and pretended that he might faint or have a heart attack. Maybe both.

"Why, if we did that, Kyle," Mr. Lemoncello had said, "we couldn't really call ourselves a library, could we?"

Kyle knew his idol was right. Libraries were supposed to be for everybody. Even jerks like Charles, who always pretended to be super polite around grown-ups—except Mr. Lemoncello.

"Not to be as nosy as Pinocchio," Mr. Lemoncello said to Sierra, "but you seemed more interested in reading your book than in marveling at my latest holographic extravaganza."

"Sorry, sir."

"Oh, there's nothing to be sorry about—a game, by the way, that I wish I had invented. I was just curious about what you were reading."

"It's called *Seabiscuit: An American Legend* by Laura Hillenbrand."

Mr. Lemoncello waggled his eyebrows, put his hand to his mouth, and hollered, "Oh, Mr. Raymo? Is there a Seabiscuit in the house?"

Suddenly, a bugle blared, a bell clanged, and two Thoroughbred racehorses, their jockeys up in the saddles, came thundering into the rotunda from the fire exit!

3

"Racing through the first turn, it's Seabiscuit leading in a surprise move!" cried the scratchy recorded voice of an old-fashioned racetrack announcer talking through his nose.

Kyle and his friends leapt out of the way as the two horses and their jockeys whipped around the rim of the rotunda as if it were a racetrack.

The breathless announcer kept going.

"Seabiscuit is in the lead by one length . . . two lengths. War Admiral is right on his heels."

Dust clouds billowed up behind the holographic horses' dirt-churning hooves.

"Down the back stretch. There goes War Admiral after him. Now the horse race is on. They're neck and neck, head and head, nose and nose. And it is either one; take your choice."

Kyle could feel the floor quaking as the two powerful horses galloped around the room.

"Go, Seabiscuit!" shouted Sierra, waving her book in the air.

"Both jockeys driving!" cried the track announcer. "It's horse against horse. Seabiscuit leads by a length. Now Seabiscuit by a length and a half. Seabiscuit by three! Seabiscuit is the winner!"

The horses vanished.

"Woo-hoo!" shouted Kyle.

"Whoa!" cried Miguel. "That was amazing!"

"That was Seabiscuit and War Admiral from their match race of 1938 at Pimlico—a racetrack near Baltimore," said Sierra.

"It was unreal," said Akimi.

"I know," said Kyle. "It was incredible!"

"No, I mean *it wasn't real*! You could see through the horses!"

"Those stupid horses scared me!" whined Andrew Peckleman, sliding his goggle-sized glasses up the bridge of his nose with one finger. "I thought they were going to run right over us. Then I realized they were just holograms!"

"Well, Andrew," said Mr. Lemoncello, "let this be a lesson to us all: The first answer isn't always the best answer. Chet?"

"Yes, sir?"

"Tell them about our brand-new Nonfictionator."

"Sorry, sir. No can do. That information is top-secret,

classified, and, I believe, restrictified. I also believe that 'restrictified' is not an actual word."

"Actually, it's a new word—one I invented and wrote down with my frindle! Plus, I hereby and forthwith—not to mention fifthwith—officially declassify and derestrictify the information in question." Mr. Lemoncello turned to the kids. "Mr. Raymo is new here at the library and somewhat shy. Perhaps, if you clap your hands as you would for Tinker Bell, we can convince him to tell us about our new Nonfictionator!"

Everybody clapped. Kyle even whistled.

"Very well." Mr. Raymo stood up and smoothed out his lab coat. "Thanks to its high-speed processor and enormous database, the Nonfictionator can generate historical holograms capable of conversing with our library patrons. Ask a question, they'll answer it. The Nonfictionator can bring historical characters to interactive life."

"With this new invention," added Mr. Lemoncello, "nonfiction doesn't have to be dry and dusty, unless, of course, it's a horse race or Lawrence of Arabia. Chet, if you please—astound me!"

"Yes, sir," said Mr. Raymo. He tapped the glass on his tablet computer.

"Careful, dear," trilled a voice from the second floor. "I smell horse poop."

"I am very familiar with horse droppings," said another.

"That's Eleanor Roosevelt," said Akimi, grabbing Kyle's arm. "She's my hero!"

13

"And Sacagawea!" added Miguel. "The Shoshone interpreter and guide from the Lewis and Clark expedition!"

The two holographic women descended a spiral staircase from the second floor.

"Go ahead," said Mr. Lemoncello. "Ask them a question."

Kyle couldn't resist. "Um, Ms. Sacagawea, how come you know so much about horse poop?"

"Because I know much about horses," she replied. "In 1805, when I was the only woman traveling with Lewis and Clark, they needed fresh horses to cross the Rockies. I helped them barter a pony deal with the nearest Shoshone tribe, whose leader turned out to be my long-lost brother, Cameahwait."

"Fascinating," said Eleanor Roosevelt. "We could've used your negotiating skills when creating the United Nations."

The two women drifted across the library floor toward one of the meeting rooms and then vanished.

"Now, *that*'s incredible," said Andrew.

Kyle snapped his fingers. "With the Nonfictionator, we could create all sorts of new exhibits where historical holograms answer questions people ask them!"

Mr. Lemoncello slapped himself in the forehead. "Why didn't I think of that? Oh, wait. I did. Several months ago."

"Is this why we're having that special board of trustees meeting this weekend?" asked Andrew. "To unveil your new invention?"

"Perhaps," said Mr. Lemoncello mischievously. "I also have a very special announcement to make. Something that will definitely keep several board members from being bored! Oh—slight change of plans. Instead of meeting here at the library, we will gather at my new home!"

He handed out flashy business cards with an address printed on them.

"You have a new house?" asked Miguel.

"Well, it's new to me! Moved in on Tuesday. I would've moved in sooner, but it took them longer than anticipated to install the floor in the living room."

"Why'd it take so long?" asked Akimi.

"Because," said Mr. Lemoncello, "it's a trampoline."

Okay, thought Kyle. Witnessing a famous horse race and chatting with historical characters was cool. But a trampoline floor?

That was going to be awesome!

4

In Kansas City, Missouri, the game-making Krinkle brothers were facing a crisis.

Their newest game was a bomb. Children hated it. Parents hated it. Sales were plummeting.

In damage-control mode, the Krinkle brothers quickly convened a focus group to find out why the new product launch had been such a failure.

The two brothers, Frederick and David, who were both well over sixty, sat in a viewing room behind a one-way mirror. Both wore suits, ties, and crisp white shirts. Both fiddled with their golden "K" cuff links.

The "respondents"—children ages ten through fifteen—and a research moderator were on the other side of the glass, seated around a long conference table.

"So are you guys ready to help us make a good game even better?" asked the chipper moderator.

The children shrugged.

"I guess," said one, whose name tag labeled him as Jack. "I mean, you guys are paying us and all."

"Good attitude!" said the moderator. "Okay, you've all had a chance to play with Whoop Dee Doodle Thirteen. Reactions? Thoughts?"

The children shrugged again.

"It's sort of boring?" said a girl named Lilly.

The other kids started nodding. "'Boring' is a good word for it," said one.

"Stupid," said a boy.

"And sad," said a girl. "It's just sad."

"It's the exact same game as Whoop Dee Doodle Twelve," added Jack. "And Whoop Dee Doodle Eleven."

In the viewing room, David Krinkle's left eye started twitching.

"That's not true," he muttered. "We put a smiley face on the whoopee cushion!"

"Ungrateful brats," mumbled Frederick, who was always a little grumpier than David.

The object of all the Krinkle brothers' Whoop Dee Doodle games was to get your teammates to guess a phrase or famous saying by using only pictures, no words. If the time in the sandglass ran out before your team guessed correctly, you had to sit on a whoopee cushion.

Whoop Dee Doodle 13 was the thirteenth edition of the game. A bright yellow starburst on the box top said it was "All New and All Fun!" The company's lawyers assured the Krinkles they could legally make that claim because the clue cards and phrases were new. So was the sandglass. It used to be pink. Now it was purple.

But customers weren't buying the claim or the game.

And it was the only new product the Krinkle brothers had in the pipeline for the coming holiday season—just six months away.

"My grandmother made me play Whoop Dee Doodle Thirteen when I was home sick from school last month," said Lilly. "It was about as much fun as the stale saltines and flat ginger ale she gave me."

"Okay, okay," said the moderator. "I'm hearing you. Let me topline these notions." He turned his back to the kids and started filling a whiteboard with words like "boring," "stupid," "sad," and "stomach flu."

While the moderator wasn't paying attention, Jack showed Lilly his smartphone.

"Have you played Mr. Lemoncello's Oh, Gee, Emoji! yet?" he whispered to her.

"No."

"Okay, let's put the phone away, Jack," said the moderator.

Jack didn't listen. "Guess the book or movie."

He showed everybody the emoji clue.

Lilly studied the phone.

The other boys and girls leaned across the table to peer at Jack's phone and try to solve the puzzle first.

 OHMY

"Got it!" said Lilly. "It's *The Wizard of Oz*!"

"Is that game fun?" asked a boy.

"Fun?" said Jack, happily imitating the tagline on every Lemoncello TV commercial. "Hello? It's a Lemoncello!"

"Enough," fumed Frederick behind the one-way mirror. "Turn them off! I hate those stupid commercials!"

David flicked the intercom switch so they wouldn't have to listen to the little monsters in the other room.

"Thirteen was bad luck," said David, his eye spasming. "That's all."

"Bad luck? It could ruin us!" Frederick was seething.

"We just need a new idea," said David. "A new game. Something spectacular. A home run!"

"We also need a way to stop Luigi Lemoncello once and for all," said Frederick, working his hands together.

"That ludicrous lunatic has been a boil on our backsides long enough."

David smirked. "The answer is simple."

"Oh, really? And how do you propose we create a new smash hit while simultaneously crushing Mr. Lemoncello's Imagination Factory?"

"Easy. We just need to increase our research and re-positioning efforts."

Frederick actually smiled. "Hmm. Too bad Benjamin Bean is no longer in our employ. He was one of the best researchers we ever hired."

"Don't worry," said David. "Our new recruit is already on the job."

"Is he up to the task?"

"Oh, yes. In fact, *she* will start this weekend!"

5

Friday night, Kyle's mother drove him to Mr. Lemoncello's home for the trustees meeting.

"I bet his house is amazing inside," said Kyle.

After the Library Olympics ended, Mr. Lemoncello had converted the main building of the Blue Jay Extended Stay Lodge, which had been Olympia Village, into a fully renovated mansion (adding a forty-foot-tall glass ceiling over the whole thing so he could see the stars at night). He kept the motel's outlying guest chalets so out-of-town trustees and their parents would always have a nice place to stay when they came to Alexandriaville for official meetings and events.

The first thing Kyle noticed when his mom pulled in was the clusters of sandbagged balloons lining the driveway.

"Balloons!" said Kyle. "I hoped there'd be balloons."

The next thing he noticed was the line of parked bookmobiles.

"I guess they picked up the out-of-towners at the airport," said Kyle.

Kyle and his mom hurried to the front door, where instead of a doorbell or knocker there was a shiny brass plaque engraved with these words: "To enter, look in the mirror and say 'emases nepo.' "

"The plaque must be the mirror," said Kyle's mom, because it was shiny enough for her to see her reflection in it.

"Emases nepo!" she said loudly.

Nothing happened.

"Wait a second," said Kyle. "It's a puzzle. If you flip the letters, like a *mirror* would, and read them backward, it says 'open sesame'!"

The instant Kyle spoke the words, the doorknob twisted and the door glided open.

Mr. Lemoncello stood on the other side.

"Welcome!" he said. He was dressed like a daredevil in bright yellow socks, a yellow flight suit, and a lemon-spangled crash helmet. "Be careful crossing the carpet in the living room, Mrs. Keeley. It's a little springy."

"I know. Kyle told me."

"Did he tell you about the bathroom?"

"No."

"It's a bouncy house. Makes using it that much more fun! So be sure to hang on to your toilet paper!"

Kyle and his mom made their way into the living room and bounded across the carpet.

"Hey, everybody—look at me!" cried Angus Harper, a kid from Texas, who'd been on the Southwest team in the Olympics. He was bouncing off the trampoline floor and leaping for the ceiling so he could try to grab one of the pairs of banana shoes dangling off the upside-down flamingo chandelier.

"Excuse me, I need something in the kitchen," said Mr. Lemoncello, sliding his feet into a pair of fuzzy slippers, which were fashioned after the fluffy frazzled birds from his video game sensation Rampaging Robin Rage.

He clicked his heels together three times and said, "To the kitchen, please!"

Four pairs of propellers twirled at the tips and heels of the slippers. Five seconds later Mr. Lemoncello rose off the floor and drifted across the room. He ducked his head under a doorjamb and disappeared.

"I have to see his kitchen!" exclaimed Kyle's mom.

"I have to have those drone slippers!" said Kyle.

They both hurried as best they could across the wobbly living room floor and into the kitchen, where they saw Mr. Lemoncello float up to retrieve a punch bowl from the highest shelf in the thirty-foot-tall pantry.

"It's just like the hover ladders in the library," said Kyle's mom.

"Except drone slippers are even better!" said Kyle.

"I want a pair," said Miguel, who was already in the

kitchen with his dad, both of them gawking at all the food being prepared by a team of chefs.

The kitchen's center island (which was shaped like Sicily) was piled high with pizza, hamburgers, hot dogs, french fries, chicken fingers, macaroni and cheese, and Hot Pockets. There was also a vegetable platter, plus a hollowed-out watermelon filled with all sorts of fruit nibbles.

Mr. Lemoncello led the team of chefs and servers into the dining room, where the legs of the massive banquet table were carved to look like the legs on a Dr. Seuss creature. Kyle's mom sat at the separate grown-ups' table (it was shorter than the one for the board of trustees). Kyle found a seat next to a girl he vaguely remembered from the Olympics. Katherine Something.

"I'm Kyle Keeley," he said, extending his hand. "I live here in Ohio."

The girl shook his hand and smiled. "I'm Katherine Kelly. From Kansas City, Missouri."

"Funny," said Kyle. "Our last names are kind of similar—so we have the same initials: KK!"

The girl laughed. "Yeah. We have something else in common, too."

"What?"

"Famous game makers live in our hometowns. You have Mr. Lemoncello; I have the Krinkle brothers!"

6

"Dinner was delicious, wouldn't you agree?" said Mr. Lemoncello, standing at the head of the very long table.

The forty or fifty kids and parents in the dining room applauded. The chefs and serving staff took a bow.

"All right," said Mr. Lemoncello. "Parents and guardians? Our security guards, Clarence and Clement, will escort you next door to the Retro Arcade, where you may play Space Invaders, Pac-Man, Donkey Kong, and all the games of your youth for free in a game center that looks—and, more important, *smells*—exactly like the mall arcades you grew up in!"

"Yee-haw!" hollered Angus Harper's father as he led the stampede of adults out of the dining room.

After they were gone, Mr. Lemoncello addressed his young trustees.

"I hereby declare this meeting of the Lemoncello

Library board of trustees officially open. I also do declare," he added in a genteel Southern accent, "that I *loved* that lemon chiffon pie! Now then, as you may have noticed, Julie of the Wolves isn't here tonight, and neither is Dr. Zinchenko. Julie is on a shelf at the library and Dr. Z is in Domodedovo, Russia, where she is celebrating her mother's birthday with pickled fish, fried cabbage dumplings, and birthday pie."

Kyle looked around the table. His friends from school—Akimi, Sierra, Miguel, and Andrew—were there, of course. But not all the members of the board of trustees could fly to Ohio for every meeting. It looked like maybe twenty other Library Olympians had made the trip, including Abia Sulayman, a very serious girl wearing a hijab, who never thought Kyle was all that funny. He also saw Diane Capriola from Georgia, Stephanie Youngerman from Idaho, and Pranav Pillai from California.

Kyle looked back to Mr. Lemoncello. He couldn't wait to hear the big announcement. He hoped it was a new game. Something as exciting as the Olympics or the escape game!

"Marjory Muldauer sends her regrets," Mr. Lemoncello said, making Kyle wait *even longer* to hear the big announcement. "Apparently, they needed her help organizing the magazine racks at the Library of Congress. Speaking of tidying things up, I would like to personally commend local board members Miguel Fernandez and

26

Andrew Peckleman, who earlier this week helped us with some archival items in the library's basement."

More applause.

"What'd you guys organize down there?" Kyle asked Miguel, who was sitting next to him.

"Just some papers and junk from the early days of Mr. Lemoncello's business career," said Miguel.

"And now for the first item on my agenda and also in my hands." Mr. Lemoncello held up what looked like a shiny black shoebox. A cluster of stubby antennas and strobing LEDs were arrayed along the top. Several gyrating satellite dishes the size of quarters rotated on the sides.

"For those of you joining us from out of town who did not witness last week's stunning demonstration at the library, I wanted to quickly introduce you to our newest funification device: the Nonfictionator! Chet? Tell them how it works!"

Mr. Raymo, the newly appointed chief imagineer, stood up.

"The box Mr. Lemoncello is currently holding in his hands is, of course, a portable, less powerful unit than the Nonfictionator at the library, which is supported by a massive network of mainframe computers."

"The box also operates as a universal remote!" said Mr. Lemoncello, tapping a red button on its side. The lights dimmed. He thumbed a scroll wheel. Violin music wafted out of the ceiling speakers. He scrolled again and somewhere a popcorn popper started popping. "It can control every electronic device in the house!"

"Simple infrared technology, actually," said Mr. Raymo modestly.

"And now," said Mr. Lemoncello, "I will use the device to dial up a holographic, interactive, and very attractive Supreme Court justice—Oliver Wendell Holmes Junior. He will administer our official Lemoncello Vow of Secrecy Oath before revealing something we need to keep secret."

"Holmes was on the court from 1902 to 1932," whispered Miguel.

"His opinions are still quoted and cited to this day," added Katherine Kelly from across the table.

"Oyez, oyez, oyez," said Mr. Lemoncello, bopping a button. "Here comes the judge."

The ghostly image of a very somber-looking man draped in black robes appeared next to Mr. Lemoncello at the head of the table. He sported a bushy walrus mustache and wore a starched shirt with a stiff collar that stood straight up.

"Now, if it please the court," Mr. Lemoncello said to the hologram, "will you kindly administer our super-duper double-pinky secrecy oath?"

Justice Holmes turned to the diners gathered around the table. "Please rise, raise your right hand, and repeat after me."

All the guests stood.

"I, insert your name."

Everybody said "I" and added their names.

Except Mr. Lemoncello.

He said, "I, insert your name."

The former Supreme Court justice cleared his throat disapprovingly.

"Oh. Right. I, Luigi Libretto Lemoncello . . ."

Justice Holmes continued: "Do solemnly swear or affirm that I will never reveal any of the secrets I am privy to as a member of this esteemed board of trustees. Cross my heart and hope to die, stick a booger in my eye."

When all the trustees quit giggling, they repeated the oath.

Mr. Lemoncello flicked off the Nonfictionator. Justice Holmes disappeared.

"Since you are all duly and officially sworn to secrecy," said Mr. Lemoncello, "how'd you like a sneak peek at what I hope will be my game company's biggest hit this holiday season?"

"Woo-hoo!" shouted Kyle.

"We'd love it!" added Angus.

"Very well," said Mr. Lemoncello. "But remember—it's a secret. Even Santa doesn't know about it yet!"

7

"Right now," said Mr. Lemoncello, "the tremendous holographic magic of the Nonfictionator only works inside the library or here in this extremely expensive portable unit. But . . ."

Mr. Lemoncello let everybody hang in suspense for a few seconds.

Finally, when Kyle thought he might burst, Mr. Lemoncello tapped the remote button on top of the Nonfictionator box.

A giant flat-screen TV brightened inside the wall behind him.

"This November," he announced, "just in time for the holiday shopping season, we will introduce what could be a real game changer of a game. Fantabulous Floating Emoji! It's like charades, except the clues are given by three-D emoticons projected over the board by the 'magic holographic eye'!"

A computer-generated animation of the game appeared on the TV screen. There was a trail of spaces winding around the edges of the board. An emerald-green disk sat in the center, between stacks of red, green, blue, and yellow cards.

"Choose a category!" said Mr. Lemoncello.

On the screen, an animated yellow card flipped over to reveal "classic children's books."

Suddenly, a three-dimensional rotating plate of spaghetti—complete with a twirling fork—floated over the board.

"That is so cool!" said Pranav.

"*Cloudy with a Chance of Meatballs*!" guessed Andrew.

Mr. Lemoncello honked like a goose. "Sorry. Incorrect. Next emoji!"

A rotating apple appeared next to the spaghetti.

"Johnny Appleseed's Italian grandmother!" guessed Akimi.

Everybody sort of looked at her.

Mr. Lemoncello goose-honked again.

A third emoji appeared over the board: a fuzzy bug.

"*Finding the Worm* by Mark Goldblatt?" said Sierra hesitantly.

This time Mr. Lemoncello just shook his head.

A fourth and fifth 3-D emoji simultaneously materialized over the game board: a hamburger and a lollipop.

"*The Very Hungry Caterpillar*!" shouted Kyle.

"Ding, ding, ding!" said Mr. Lemoncello. "We have a winner!"

"Yes!" Kyle arm-pumped in triumph.

"Way to go, bro," said Miguel.

Mr. Lemoncello bopped a button on his boxy controller, and the screen went blank.

"We are all set to begin production next week so that this holiday season kids everywhere can bring home their own hologram projector at a reasonable price. It's so cheap even my family could've afforded it. And we were so poor we used to eat cereal with a fork to save money on milk!"

Everyone laughed.

"Thank you," said Mr. Lemoncello. "I'm here all week." He brandished a rolled-up tube of blueprints. "And these are the incredibletastic new game's complete design schematics."

He bent down and pulled back the rug to reveal a floor safe.

"Should I not be able, for whatever reason, to fulfill my duties as head of the Imagination Factory, I want you, my trusted trustees, to pick up the torch and carry on. Not that I want you to burn these blueprints to make a torch, mind you, because you will need them to build the board game. You will also need to know the combination to this floor safe. Kindly keep it a secret, too, for it is the same series of random letters I use all the time: R right. E left. A right. D left. That's right. There's nothing left. It's just R-E-A-D. The key to unlocking everything in the universe!"

Across the table, Katherine Kelly was writing the combination down in her small notebook. Kyle didn't need to. He could memorize four letters. Heck, anybody could.

"So much for fun and games," said Mr. Lemoncello. "Let's move on to the next item on our agenda. Lemoncello Library business."

Sierra, Pranav, and Andrew clapped.

Kyle wanted to play another round of Fantabulous Floating Emoji or hear the exciting announcement Mr. Lemoncello had promised he was going to make. Library business sounded boring.

"It's time for my major announcement!" said Mr. Lemoncello.

Woo-hoo, thought Kyle. So much for being bored. It was showtime!

"To thank you all for your dedicated service," said Mr. Lemoncello, "I have created a brand-new, board-members-only board game—without a board!"

Kyle leapt out of his seat. "Yes!"

He pumped both fists over his head.

Everybody else just stared at him.

"Sorry."

Kyle sat back down.

"No need to apologize, Mr. Keeley!" exclaimed Mr. Lemoncello. "For I am as excited as you are. Now then, where was I? Ah, yes. My dining room. But this game will take you far, far away from here! And if you win, it will take you even farther—on a tour of libraries all across North America!"

Now Kyle was super excited. He and his family had never really done much traveling. Except to Disney World. Once.

Oh, they'd also been to Cedar Point, an amusement park in Ohio. Kyle tried to forget that trip. His brother Curtis had thrown up on the Corkscrew roller coaster. Kyle was in the seat in front of him.

"What's this new game called?" asked Akimi.

Before he replied, Mr. Lemoncello struck a finger-pointed-to-the-sky pose, just like his statue in the fountain in the lobby of the library—only there wasn't any water spurting out of his mouth.

"Mr. Lemoncello's Fabulous Fact-Finding Frenzy!"

Angus Harper's hand shot up.

"Yes, Angus?"

"Are you sure it's a game, sir? Finding facts sounds an awful lot like a homework assignment."

"Oh, it's a game, all right," said Mr. Lemoncello. "Perhaps the most challenging one any of you will ever play. That's why the prize is so amazerrific. And why only ten of you will even have a chance of winning it!"

8

All the trustees were buzzing excitedly.

Mr. Lemoncello tapped the side of his water glass with a spoon to regain everyone's attention.

"The Fabulous Fact-Finding Frenzy will consist of two rounds," he announced. "The first elimination round I like to call 'the elimination round,' because it is the round in which players will be eliminated. You will be paired up in two-person teams as we endeavor to see who amongst you is most like Mike Mulligan with his steam shovel and knows how to dig, dig, dig. The top five teams, consisting of ten players total, will move on to round two. The rest of you will be sent home with lovely parting gifts."

"What's the second round, sir?" asked Pranav Pillai.

"Ah! Good question, Pranav."

"Thank you, sir."

"The second round will come after the first one and last a few days, so you might need to miss some school. . . ."

"Woo-hoo!" shouted Kyle, doing a quick raise-the-roof dance move.

Everyone else stared at him. They were mostly brainiacs. Not that there was anything wrong with that. They just seemed to enjoy going to school, doing homework, and memorizing math junk more than Kyle did.

"The second round of the game," Mr. Lemoncello continued, "is the actual Fact-Finding Frenzy! In it, our top ten research assistants will race against each other to see who can solve clues, unravel puzzles, pass through roadblocks, and overcome any and all obstacles to find the fascinating fact we're looking for!"

Kyle was super excited. This new game reminded him of that TV show where contestants raced each other around the world. It was one of his faves.

"The facts," Mr. Lemoncello continued, "will be linked to the five new interactive Nonfictionator displays we're creating for the library. Displays that will be revealed to the public at a grand gala featuring cake, balloons, indoor fireworks, confetti cannons, and a surprise guest appearance by the one and only Haley Daley!"

Everybody cheered.

Haley had been one of the winners in the first escape game but had since moved out to Hollywood, where she was now a TV and singing star on the Disney Channel.

"Who are the five historical figures to be honored with new exhibits?" asked Stephanie Youngerman from Idaho.

"Those names will not be revealed until round two," said Mr. Lemoncello. "We're still tweaking the list."

Mr. Lemoncello went on to explain that the library lobby would be home base, just like the home square from his first big hit, the board game Family Frenzy, which he invented when he was still a teenager. It was the game that earned the bazillionaire his first millions.

The teams in round two would race each other—out into the field and back to the library.

"You may need to travel on planes, trains, and automobiles," said Mr. Lemoncello. "Not to worry. Our fleet of bookmobiles will be at your disposal—as will my corporate jets, airplanes, and helicopters. So be sure your parents or guardians sign these permission slips."

He handed out tightly rolled-up scrolls of paper.

"They're kind of long," muttered Andrew after opening his.

"Oh, yes," said Mr. Lemoncello. "Because they cover everything—even stuff I haven't thought of yet!"

Akimi raised her hand.

"So what does the winning team actually win?" she asked.

"Something more priceless than a million dollars, because let's face it, a million dollars has a price: one million dollars. If you win, you will tour the country with these holographic exhibits and see North America—for free!"

"Wait a second," whined Andrew Peckleman. "I thought these new exhibits were for *our* library, downtown."

"At first," said Mr. Lemoncello. "Then, in the fall, we will take the Nonfictionator and our team of fabulous fact finders on the road to libraries all over North America! Whoever wins will have an all-expenses-paid trip to see Washington, Chicago, New York, Seattle, Vancouver, and San Francisco, where you will be greeted as library rock stars! But wait, there's more. The two members of the winning team will also be the first two people in the whole entire world—including Antarctica—to take home my new Fantabulous Floating Emoji game the instant it rolls off the assembly line!"

Kyle's heart started beating a little faster.

It always did that whenever he wanted to win, win, win!

9

"We're from out of town," David Krinkle said to the holographic research librarian stationed behind her desk in the Rotunda Reading Room.

"We'd like to do a little research," added his brother, Frederick, clutching a flat briefcase with combination-lock clasps.

"So I assumed," said the research librarian. She pointed to the illuminated sign over her head:

ADRIENNE WAINTRAUB, RESEARCH LIBRARIAN
I may not know everything, but I know how to find it.

"We hope we're not too late," said David.

"The library is open until ten p.m. on Fridays," said Ms. Waintraub without any emotion, because her interface was strictly data-driven.

"We would've been here sooner, but we had to fly to Detroit and then rent a car," explained Frederick. "Too bad this sleepy little burg doesn't have a proper airport."

"Actually," said the holographic librarian, "Alexandriaville is served by the Wood County Regional Airport. Although no commercial carriers operate out of the facility, it is home to many general aviation aircraft and is a destination for corporate aircraft doing business in the region."

David leaned forward. "Tell me, Miss Waynetree . . ."

"The proper pronunciation of my name is WINE-trowb. It is a Jewish-German surname meaning 'grape.' My ancestor Abraham Waintraub's name can be found on the New York arriving-passenger lists of 1824."

"Very impressive research," said Frederick, sounding anything but impressed.

"Research is my job, Mr. FREDERICK KRINKLE."

"What? How do you know my name?"

"I am equipped with facial recognition software."

"So you know who I am, too?" said David.

"Yes, DAVID KRINKLE. You two, together, are the Krinkle brothers, the game makers. You have a combined net worth of three hundred million dollars. You make most of the dominoes, marbles, pachisi, and Chinese checkers sets sold in America and Canada. You are considered Mr. Lemoncello's chief domestic rivals in the toy and game-manufacturing sectors of the United States economy."

"So?" bristled Frederick. "Are you going to toss us out

of the loony old bat's loopy library just because we're his main competitors?"

"No," said the flickering hologram. "This is a public facility. All are welcome here. Also I am a hologram, a three-dimensional projection of a photographic image. As such, I cannot toss anything. Excuse me. One moment. Data loading. Data loading."

Her eyeballs turned into spinning pinwheels for a few seconds.

"Your most popular game to date is Whoop Dee Doodle, versions one through thirteen, which, according to *Game Maker* magazine, was a 'Whopper of a Dee-saster.' Your cat's name, when you were growing up, was Lucifer. You like the crusts cut off your toast, soft-boiled eggs—"

"How can you possibly know all that?" demanded Frederick.

"I am a research librarian. Knowing things is what I do."

"You sound like a robot!" exclaimed David.

"Yes. Because I am. A robot. My name was given to me by Mr. Lemoncello in an attempt to humanize my interface and to honor the research librarian at the New York Public Library who, in the early years of his career, gave him assistance, guidance, and all the answers he ever sought."

"Is Luigi here?" asked Frederick, his eyes darting back and forth nervously.

"No. He is at his home. Entertaining his board of trustees."

"Oh, too bad," said David. "Can you tell us where we might find the so-called Lemoncello-abilia Room? We'd like to examine some of the artifacts from Luigi's past."

Ms. Waintraub's eyes grew wide. Her pupils dilated. She leaned forward and projected a 3-D animated display of the library's multilevel floor plan above the reference desk.

"You will find THE LEMONCELLO-ABILIA ROOM on the third floor," she said as a blinking line of dots illustrated the shortest route. "It is conveniently located right next to THE ART AND ARTIFACTS ROOM. You may access the upper levels of the library via the spiral staircases, the elevator, or—if you have the proper mountain-climbing gear and will sign a liability waiver—the hover ladders."

"We'll take the elevator," snarled Frederick.

"The Lemoncello-abilia Room will close in fifteen minutes," said the hologram.

"We'll be quick," said David. "Come on, Frederick."

Frederick hugged the briefcase tightly to his chest as the brothers bustled over to the elevator and rode it up to the third floor to do what they had flown to Ohio to do.

Kyle couldn't wait for the new game to begin.

But he had to.

The elimination round wouldn't take place until the following weekend. A lot of the board members had to fly home to go to school, but most would be flying back to Ohio on Friday morning for the start of the new competition that night.

Kyle had to go to school, too.

On Monday, in social studies, he was supposed to give an oral report on his "favorite famous figure."

Of course, he chose Mr. Lemoncello.

He concentrated on the billionaire game inventor's early childhood in Alexandriaville, Ohio.

"When he was our age," Kyle told the class, "young Luigi Lemoncello loved the public library because, with nine brothers and sisters—all of them crammed into a

tiny apartment with only one bathroom—the Alexandriaville public library was the only place where he could go
to—and I quote from an interview he gave to NPR last
year—'hear myself think and work on my game ideas.'"

All in all, Kyle did extremely well. His teacher, Mrs.
Cameron, even congratulated him for "citing his sources."
Kyle was certain he'd aced it.

Unfortunately, Charles Chiltington gave his report
right after Kyle. Charles was dressed in his usual school
uniform (one that nobody else ever wore): a blue blazer,
khaki pants, white shirt, and striped tie. He looked like he
thought middle school was a formal dance at his father's
country club. He also had a slim laptop computer tucked
under his arm.

"Is it permissible for me to do a PowerPoint talk, Mrs.
Cameron?" he asked sweetly. "I think presentation software helps to augment and enrich what could otherwise
seem exceedingly tedious and dreary if presented in the
somniferous mode of a traditional oral report."

"Of course, Charles," said Mrs. Cameron. She was one
of the teachers who totally fell for Charles's smarmy rou-
tine and loved all the big words he used.

"Thank you, Mrs. Cameron. And may I say, your
new glasses frame the work of art that is your face quite
wondrously."

"Why, thank you, Charles. Please, proceed."

Chiltington hooked up his laptop to the Smart Board
and blew the class away with a slide-show presentation

that included awesome animations, video clips, and transitions. It was all about John Pierpont Morgan, a famous American financier, banker, and all-around rich guy who used to buy all sorts of stuff, like Charles Dickens's original manuscripts and Michelangelo's sketches, to put on display in his private library.

"Very impressive, Mr. Chiltington," said Mrs. Cameron when he was done. "That's what I call an A-plus-plus-plus presentation."

"Thank you, Mrs. Cameron," said Charles. "But as you've often instructed us, anything worth doing is worth doing well!"

The bell rang.

The class filed out the door.

"That's two for me and none for you!" Charles sneered the second they hit the hall. He laughed and strutted away.

Kyle felt the way his big brother Mike probably did when he missed a jump shot at the final buzzer and his basketball team lost by one point.

Only that never happened.

Mike's basketball teams always finished their seasons undefeated.

And his brainiac brother Curtis always got straight A's.

After two defeats to Chiltington in a row, Kyle now held the family title of the Biggest Loser.

11

"Come on," Kyle called to his mom at seven-thirty on Friday night. "I don't want to be late!"

All week long, Kyle had been dreaming about winning Mr. Lemoncello's exclusive, board-members-only board-game-without-a-board. His mom drove him downtown to the library, where he joined twenty-four other Library Olympians under the Wonder Dome at eight o'clock sharp (when the library closed early for the special event).

"Text me when you need to be picked up," said Kyle's mom.

"Will do! Thanks for the ride."

He hurried up the front steps, raced across the lobby, and skidded into the Rotunda Reading Room, where he met up with his friends.

"Check out the statues," said Miguel, nodding toward the recessed nooks between the rotunda's ten arched windows.

It was a good thing that the holographic sculptures stood on top of glowing pedestals where their names were inscribed, because Kyle only recognized a few: Marie Curie, Albert Einstein, and Galileo Galilei. He had no idea who the others were: Dian Fossey, Jacobus Arminius, Jane Goodall, Neil deGrasse Tyson, Isaac Newton, Louis Pasteur, and Nicolaus Copernicus.

"They're all famous researchers," said Akimi, whose dad was an engineer. Akimi knew science the way Sierra knew books.

Suddenly, the Wonder Dome blossomed into a swirling, animated version of the cover to the Beatles' famous *Sgt. Pepper's Lonely Hearts Club Band* album. A bouncy version of "With a Little Help from My Friends" filled the rotunda.

Mr. Lemoncello appeared in a spotlight on the second-floor balcony. He was dressed in a shiny blue marching-band uniform with tassels and boards on the shoulders—just like Paul McCartney in the famous album cover photo.

"Cheerio and greetings to you all!" Mr. Lemoncello decreed from his lofty perch. "I'm delighted that so many of you chose to act like books and have returned to the library! For this elimination round, you will need the higher power of lucky plus a little help from your friends. So please—pair up!"

Akimi and Kyle immediately locked eyes.

"Team?" they said simultaneously.

"Team!" They shook on it.

"If it's science junk . . . ," said Kyle.

"I'll take the lead," said Akimi. "And, Kyle? We just call it science. Not science junk."

"Right. Gotcha."

As Mr. Lemoncello drifted down a spiral staircase, his shimmering boots, complete with tall accordion heels, played along with the bouncy bass line of the Beatles tune.

"Tonight's elimination-round game," he announced when he reached the floor and the music stopped, "is titled Who or What in the World Are We?" He twirled in place (which made his accordion shoes wheeze like a deflating bagpipe sack) and faced Ms. Waintraub, the holographic research librarian, who had just appeared behind her desk.

"Adrienne?" said Mr. Lemoncello, doing his best to sound like a game show host. "Tell them how we play!"

"Tonight's category will be 'famous foursomes,' " she said in her bored computer voice.

"Wow," mumbled Miguel, who had teamed up with Abia Sulayman, "she's a load of laughs."

"She is serious because research is a serious proposition," said Abia.

"Does it have to be *that* serious?" joked Kyle.

"Yes, Kyle Keeley. Research requires due diligence and proper perseverance."

"You see why I teamed up with her?" said Miguel with a grin. "We're gonna rock this round!"

"The Beatles, of course, were a famous foursome," continued the research librarian.

49

"In fact," added Mr. Lemoncello, "when I was your age, we called the Beatles the Fab Four, because they were fabulous and there were four of them—not because they resembled a multipack of laundry detergent."

"You will each be given a different foursome to identify," droned Ms. Waintraub. "Each clue card will lead you to one of the four items in your grouping. When you correctly identify your first item, you will be given a clue to help you find the second. At any point in the clue-giving-and-taking process, you can guess what the four persons, places, or things have in common. However, should you guess incorrectly, you will be eliminated from the competition."

"And that," exclaimed Mr. Lemoncello, "is precisely why we call this the elimination round! Please step forward and receive your first clues."

The twelve teams stepped up one at a time, and each took a bright yellow envelope from Mr. Lemoncello.

"Do not open your envelopes until I say when. Of course, I don't know when I might say when. Oh, dear. I just did. Twice!"

All the teams ripped open their envelopes. Kyle and Akimi read what was written on theirs:

The past tense of "921 is"

"What?" said Kyle. "How can a number have a past tense?"

"It's a riddle, not a question," said Akimi. "If it was a question, there'd be a question mark!"

"Okay. The past tense of nine-two-one is nine-two-lost."

"Kyle, there is no past tense for the number one."

"Sure, if you want to get technical about it . . ."

"This is research. We have to—"

Akimi was cut off by Angus, who'd just slammed his palm down on the reference desk. Hard.

"Our famous foursome is card suits," he said.

"Can you show us your work?" asked Ms. Waintraub.

"No problem. Our clue was a math problem. The answer was 616.21."

"That, of course," said his teammate, Katherine, referring to notes she must've written down in her little black book, "is also the Dewey decimal classification for books about cardiology, the study of hearts."

"And," explained Angus, "since this is a Lemoncello game, we figured 'cardiology' could also be a pun referring to the study of, you know, cards. Hearts is one of four suits in every deck."

"The others are clubs, spades, and diamonds," added Katherine.

"Congratulicitations!" cried Mr. Lemoncello. "We have our first team of data diggers! Since there will be only five new exhibits, there are only four slots remaining! Work your clues, super sleuths! Work them with voracious rapidity!"

"Come on," said Akimi.

"Where are we going?" asked Kyle.

"Upstairs. Our clue is a Dewey decimal number, too!"

12

As they dashed up the spiral staircase to the Dewey decimal rooms, Kyle felt a familiar surge of adrenaline.

His competitive juices were definitely flowing again.

They reached the landing on the second floor and hurried around the wide circular balcony, sprinting for the distant door that would take them into the 900s room, which was filled with all the books from (and exhibits about) that category of the Dewey decimal system.

"The nine hundreds are for history and geography, right?" said Kyle.

"Correct," said Akimi as they rounded the bend outside the 700s door.

"So in geography, our famous foursome could be the four continents."

"There are seven of those, Kyle."

"True. But you need four to get to seven."

"Kyle?"

"Yeah?"

"You're jumping to conclusions."

"Because I want to jump into the winner's circle with Angus and Katherine!"

"Conclusion-jumping is the opposite of doing research."

Akimi grabbed the handle of the 900s room door.

"The past tense of '921 is' could be '921 was,'" she said as quickly as she could. "That would put us in the biography section."

"Why?"

"Because 921 through 928 is the range reserved as an optional location for biographies," said Akimi.

"Says who?"

"Librarians everywhere. Don't you remember studying that for the Olympics?"

"That was months ago. I already forgot all that stuff we had to memorize back then."

"Well, I didn't." She led the way into the 900s room. Since the 910s were all about travel, there were several different model airplanes and jets spinning in circles under the ceiling. Akimi marched past all the tour guidebooks and went straight to the 920s.

"Within 921," she said, "books are shelved alphabetically by a subject's last name."

"Fine. So who was Was?"

Akimi pulled "921 Was" off the shelf. "George Washington."

"Excellent. Okay. That means our famous foursome is tall presidents."

"Whaaa?"

"From that game last week, remember?"

"Kyle . . ."

"Okay. Forget tall presidents. Washington is one of four presidents with states named after them."

"No," said Akimi. "Washington's the only one."

"Okay, okay. How about presidents with their faces on money."

"Kyle?"

"Yeah?"

"We need to go downstairs and pick up our second clue and come up with a logical correlation."

"A what?"

"A *real* reason the clues go together!"

Kyle reluctantly agreed because the clock was ticking and no way was he losing two games at the library in less than two weeks.

They raced back to the first floor just in time to hear Miguel and Abia name *their* famous foursome: "The Teenage Mutant Ninja Turtles!"

"Who, of course," added Abia, sounding like she was going for extra credit points, "were named after the renowned Renaissance artists Leonardo, Michelangelo, Raphael, and Donatello."

"Congratulicitations!" shouted Mr. Lemoncello. "That means two of our five research assistant slots are now filled! Only three more to go."

Hands trembling because they knew they were falling behind, Kyle and Akimi ripped open their second clue.

This president's personal library of approximately
six thousand books became the basis of the
Library of Congress. His books were
purchased from him for $23,950.

"It's Thomas Jefferson," whispered Akimi.

"How can you know that?"

"I just do! Come on, back to the second floor."

They clanged up the spiral staircase again.

"Wait a second," said Kyle. "Jefferson was the third president, right?"

"Yes," said Akimi. "Washington, Adams, Jefferson, Madison—"

"So that's our foursome!" said Kyle, as they tore past the travel section again. "The first four presidents of the United States."

"Good guess," said Akimi, scanning the presidential biographies, hoping to find some sort of third clue. "But why didn't they do Washington, then Adams, *then* Jefferson?"

"Because Mr. Lemoncello is like me. His mind is kind of scattered and all over the place!"

"We should go back and get our third clue card," said Akimi, frantically searching the shelves. "There's nothing up here."

"I wondered why we raced up here, since we already had the answer."

"I just thought . . ."

Kyle saw something over Akimi's shoulder in the travel section. Actually, he saw *somebody*—a hologram of Teddy Roosevelt. Kyle recognized him from all those *Night at the Museum* movies.

"You made the right call," Kyle said to Akimi, nodding to the semitransparent president behind her.

Roosevelt was examining a travel book about Africa.

"Bully," he said. "I am quite fond of the West African proverb 'Speak softly and carry a big stick; you will go far!' Bully!" Then Roosevelt addressed Kyle and Akimi directly. "This third clue has been provided courtesy of the Nonfictionator."

Roosevelt saluted and disappeared.

"George Washington, Thomas Jefferson, Theodore Roosevelt," said Kyle. "Who are we missing?"

"Abraham Lincoln!" shouted Akimi. "Our Famous Foursome are the four presidents on Mount Rushmore!"

They bolted out of the 900s room.

Sped along the balcony.

Down below, two people cheered, "Woo-hoo!"

It sounded to Kyle like another pair of winners.

How many slots were left? One? Two?

He and Akimi raced down the steps.

Flew across the floor.

And waited their turn behind Sierra and Pranav, who were already addressing the research librarian.

"Our answer is the Houses of Hogwarts," said Sierra.

"And," added Pranav, "we would like to thank the Nonfictionator for sending along the holographic J. K. Rowling as our third clue."

"Congratulicitations!" cried Mr. Lemoncello. "Your answer is correct. We now have our fifth and final team of fact-finding data diggers!"

13

"But . . ."

"Sorry, Mr. Keeley," said Mr. Lemoncello. "You and Miss Hughes were the *sixth* team to report to the reference desk. We're only looking for five because we're only doing five new exhibits."

"Our famous foursome was Mount Rushmore," mumbled Akimi.

"We know that," said the super-serious research librarian. "We know all the answers."

"And," said Mr. Lemoncello, "we also know you two were—and will forever remain—the first runners-up!"

Kyle couldn't believe it. He was the board of trustees' biggest gamer, and he wouldn't even be playing the main game? That just wasn't right. Of course, he had no one to blame but himself. He'd kept slowing Akimi down. She probably would've finished in the top five if she'd flown solo.

"Thanks," said Kyle. "And thanks for the third clue from the Nonfictionator. That was neat."

"We gave one of those to every team," reported Ms. Waintraub. "It seemed only fair."

Overhead, the Wonder Dome was filled with floating images of the first five Famous Foursomes: the suits of cards, the Teenage Mutant Ninja Turtles, the yellow-brick-road travelers from *The Wizard of Oz* (Dorothy, the Scarecrow, the Tin Woodman, and the Cowardly Lion), the four sides of a ship (bow, stern, starboard, port), and, of course, the Houses of Hogwarts (Gryffindor, Ravenclaw, Hufflepuff, Slytherin).

Drifting along the bottom rim of the dome like the news scroll on a TV screen were the names of the "Top Ten Research Assistants": Diane Capriola, Jamal Davis, Miguel Fernandez, Angus Harper, Katherine Kelly, Andrew Peckleman, Pranav Pillai, Sierra Russell, Elliott Schilpp, and Abia Sulayman.

All the Alexandriaville kids had made the cut.

All except Kyle and Akimi. They'd be going home.

"Way to go," Kyle said to Miguel, knocking knuckles. "You too, Andrew."

"Don't punch me!" shrieked Andrew when he saw Kyle's raised fist. "It's not my fault you lost."

"I know," said Kyle, lowering his hand. "It was mine."

"Yes," said Akimi. "It was."

"I kept jumping to bad conclusions."

"Yes," said Akimi. "You did."

"You're never going to let me off the hook for this one, are you, Akimi?"

"No. I'm not."

"Thank you all for playing!" announced Mr. Lemoncello. "And congratulations once again to our ten winners. Your Fabulous Fact-Finding Frenzy will start tomorrow morning, here in the rotunda, before the library is open to the public, at eight o'clock sharp unless it's foggy—then it will be eight o'clock dull."

One of the shoulder boards on Mr. Lemoncello's band uniform started blinking bright red.

"Sorry," he said. "That's the hotline, direct from Moscow. I have to answer that."

Kyle heard the rip of Velcro as Mr. Lemoncello pulled the phone off his shoulder.

"Hello, Yanina! How is your mother's birthday party progressing? Have you cut the pickled fish pie yet?"

Mr. Lemoncello drifted off into the Book Nook Café to continue his conversation with the world-famous librarian Dr. Yanina Zinchenko. Ms. Waintraub addressed the winners and losers under the dome.

"Those of you who lost . . ."

Kyle wondered why she had to look directly at him when she said that.

". . . will find airplane tickets and travel vouchers waiting for you in your rooms at Mr. Lemoncello's guest chalets. Unless, like Mr. Keeley and Miss Hughes, you live here in Ohio. Then you will just go home with lovely parting gifts."

"I'm sorry I lost this for us," Kyle whispered to Akimi.

"You're forgiven," she said. "Barely."

Finally, they both smiled.

"We'll get 'em next time," said Akimi.

And before Kyle could say, "If there is a next time," Mr. Lemoncello flew through the Book Nook Café door.

"Stop the presses, hold your horses, and hang on to your hats! Not all at the same time, of course. That might prove dangerous. You'd need both hands to hang on to those ponies, so—*WHOOSH!*—there goes your hat. I've just received an urgent phone call from our head librarian, who, as you know, is visiting family in Russia this week. She insists that a sixth name be added to the list of new exhibits. Not only that, but her mother concurs. In fact, when Dr. Zinchenko's mother was blowing out the candles on her pickled fish pie, she made a wish and told everybody, because apparently in Russia that isn't against the rules."

He caught his breath.

"Anyway, at the insistence of all the Zinchenkos, foreign and domestic, we will add a sixth name to the exhibit list. That means we need six teams of research assistants, not just five. Kyle and Akimi? Congratulicitations. You were the sixth team to correctly identify your famous foursome.

61

Thereforesome, since we are now doing *six* exhibits, you two will also be moving on to the next round!"

YESSSSSSSS!

Kyle had just pulled a "Free Spin" card. Thanks to Dr. Zinchenko's mother, he was no longer eliminated. He was moving on to the big show.

He hugged Akimi, but only for a second. Then he slapped her a high five because that's what best friends do.

"Who, may I ask," said Ms. Waintraub, "is our sixth famous person?"

"Me! Luigi L. Lemoncello! I told Dr. Zinchenko, 'There's already enough Lemoncello in the Lemoncello Library,' but she insisted. Said we needed an interactive hologram of *me*. One that patrons could pepper with pertinent questions."

"That is so awesome!" cried Kyle. "In round two, I definitely want to research you!"

"Dr. Zinchenko thought you would," said Mr. Lemoncello. "And you might get that chance. Especially since you will be partnered with . . . let's see . . ."

Mr. Lemoncello scanned the faces of the eleven other players who would be moving on.

"Ah, yes. Perfect. Abia Sulayman!"

"But I was kind of hoping I could keep working with Akimi. . . ."

"You've already done that. I like to mix things up. Because the same old, same old isn't just the same and old—it's also boring."

"B-b-but . . ."

Mr. Lemoncello cut off Kyle's stammering with an arched eyebrow. "Dr. Zinchenko and I were both hoping you'd want to continue playing, Kyle. However, if you'd rather sit this game out . . ."

Kyle looked at Akimi.

She shrugged. "It's cool by me."

He looked at Abia.

She didn't look so happy.

Kyle turned to Mr. Lemoncello. "I'm in, sir!"

"Wondermous!"

14

On Saturday morning, Kyle and his new partner, Abia Sulayman, met in the Book Nook Café.

Kyle was dressed according to the instructions texted to all twelve data dashers: "Wear comfortable clothes. Something to run around in. Perhaps a tracksuit but without the track tie."

He'd chosen sweatpants, a sweatshirt, and running shoes.

Abia, however, was wearing a peasant-style blouse over a long-sleeved shirt, jeans, and a hijab—the veil covering her head and chest. It was decorated with tiny roses and completely hid all of her hair.

"Um, good morning," said Kyle. "I, uh, like your scarf."

"It is called a hijab, Kyle Keeley. Many Muslim girls wear one."

"I know. I mean I've seen some at school. I sometimes wear a baseball cap. . . ."

Abia glared at him. "I am not pleased that Mr. Lemoncello has paired us together, Kyle Keeley."

"Because I beat you in that flying dinosaur race during the Olympics?"

Now she rolled her eyes. "Pterodactyls were not dinosaurs."

"Well, they kind of looked dinosaurish. . . ."

"This is your problem, Kyle Keeley. You make assumptions. You go for the easy answer. These skills will not serve us well in a research-based competition."

She went back to eating her yogurt.

Kyle dunked a jelly doughnut into his hot cocoa as his eyes drifted around the room to study the competition.

Akimi was teamed up with Angus Harper, the scrappy kid from Texas. They were yukking it up over bowls of cereal. Angus was hanging a spoon off his nose and making Akimi laugh. That used to be Kyle's job.

Sierra Russell was with Jamal Davis, a bright kid from Seattle who wore thick black-rimmed glasses. They kept passing books back and forth across their table, reading favorite passages and completely ignoring their chocolate croissants.

Elliott Schilpp, the skinny boy from Maryland who loved to eat, and Katherine Kelly, the girl from Missouri, were *NUM-NUM-NUM*ing their way through a tray stacked with doughnuts, bagels, muffins, croissants, and hard-boiled eggs.

Miguel and Pranav Pillai, who'd been on the West Coast team at the Library Olympics, were swapping library stories.

"When I was young," said Miguel, "I once mis-shelved a human anatomy book in the insects section. I thought it was a book about ants!"

The two laughed so hard, chocolate milk came squirting out of their noses.

Andrew Peckleman, who whined a lot but definitely knew his way around a library, was teamed up with Diane Capriola, from Georgia, who could ace any riddle you tossed her way.

"I wish you were Sierra Russell," Andrew complained, sliding his glasses into place.

"And I wish you'd stop doing that slidey thing with your glasses," said Diane.

Kyle's eyes drifted back to Abia.

She was scowling at him and shaking her head.

"This is so unfair," she sighed. "How did I end up with you?"

Finally they had something in common. Because Kyle was thinking the exact same thing.

"Will all fact finders kindly report to the Rotunda Reading Room?" purred a soothing female voice from the ceiling speakers. "Thank you."

Everyone grabbed their final bites, placed their trash in the appropriate recycling bins, and hurried out the door.

Mr. Lemoncello, flanked by the security guards Clarence and Clement, stood in the center of the rotunda, waiting.

He was wearing long black robes with a white pilgrim collar and a fake white beard. He held a brass telescope and looked like an astronomer from the Middle Ages. Overhead, the Wonder Dome was filled with spinning planets and the sparkling constellations of the night sky.

"Good morning!" said Mr. Lemoncello. "Why am I dressed like Galileo Galilei, whose last name is almost the same as his first and, like Old MacDonald, has a lot of e-i, e-i, o action going on? Because as an icebreaker to help you new teammates learn to work together, we will play a quick picture puzzler. The answer is a famous quote by Galileo. When you know the answer, rush up to Ms. Waintraub and tell it to her. The order of your answers will determine the order of your departures in our amazingly awesome research race."

Mr. Lemoncello clapped his hands. The research librarian materialized behind her desk, and the Wonder Dome's stars and planets dissolved into a giant, complex rebus puzzle:

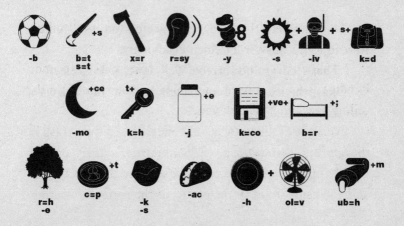

Kyle scanned the dome. Worked the puzzle in his head.

"I've got this," he announced.

"Are you certain?" said Abia. "Perhaps there will be a penalty for a wrong guess."

"Mr. Lemoncello didn't mention one," said Kyle.

"That doesn't matter. There are always consequences for faulty logic. . . ."

"My logic isn't faulty. It's a rebus. I play Mr. Lemoncello's Amazingly Baffling Picture Puzzlers all the time! Come on."

"But . . ."

Kyle rolled his eyes, grabbed a stubby pencil and a slip of paper, and wrote down his answer.

"Here," he said, showing her what he had written. "Check my work."

"ALL TRUTHS ARE EASY TO UNDERSTAND ONCE THEY ARE DISCOVERED; THE POINT IS TO DISCOVER THEM."

Abia studied the images projected on the ceiling. Reread Kyle's answer. Nodded grudgingly.

"That seems to be correct. Well done, Kyle Keeley."

Okay, the ice wasn't completely broken. But at least it was starting to defrost.

15

"Greatastic job, everyone!" cried Mr. Lemoncello after the five other teams had given the correct answer to Ms. Waintraub maybe two minutes after Kyle and Abia had given theirs.

"We beat the best of the best!" Kyle said to Abia.

"Indeed," said Abia. "But I suspect the rest of this game will not be so easy."

"Easy?" said Kyle. "I thought that rebus was pretty complicated. . . ."

"It was a childish game, Kyle Keeley. This is why you excelled at it."

Oh-kay, thought Kyle. *So much for a major thaw.*

Mr. Lemoncello whipped off his fake Galileo beard and ripped open his robes to reveal a bright yellow tracksuit decorated with tiny brown cellos.

"Now that we're all warmed up—because, trust me,

that robe and Santa beard will make anybody sweat—it's time to reveal the six names for new Lemoncello-style exhibits here at the library. The historical figures have been chosen with tremendous care, even though they will appear, at first blush, to be a random assortment of greatness or a great assortment of randomness. Voice in the ceiling? Tell us who we'll be investigating."

"You mean 'whom,' " said the ceiling lady.

"Perhaps I do," said Mr. Lemoncello. "I'm never one hundred percent certain what I mean. Drumroll, please."

Drums rolled, trumpets blared, and every time a cymbal crashed, the ceiling lady announced a new name. When she did, their picture drifted across the Wonder Dome:

"Thomas Alva Edison! Michael Jordan! Emily Dickinson! Abraham Lincoln! Orville and Wilbur Wright! And our last-minute addition, courtesy of Dr. Zinchenko: Luigi Libretto Lemoncello!"

"What do they all have in common?" mused Abia.

"It doesn't really matter," said Kyle. "That's not part of the game. . . ."

"Still, I am curious. Aren't you?"

"No. Not unless it helps us win."

"Voice in the ceiling?" cried Mr. Lemoncello. "Will you kindly read the rules because, come on—what's a game without rules except a crazy collection of cardboard, dice, and plastic playing pieces?"

"This race," cooed the smooth voice, "is intended solely for the private use of Mr. Lemoncello as an aid to help him find whom amongst you are the most fabulous fact finders. The race will not be open to the public or the press, but the Grand Gala next Saturday night will be open to all. Teams will be eliminated during each leg of the race. The winning team members, the last researchers standing, will both go on an extensive North American tour with the exhibits and take home the very first copies of Mr. Lemoncello's Fantabulous Floating Emoji hologram game!"

"Coming soon to a toy store near you!" added Mr. Lemoncello.

"The winning team will also be honored at the Grand Gala one week from tonight, when our new exhibits will first go on display!"

"Will there be cake?" asked Kyle.

"And ice cream," said the ceiling.

"Booyah!"

"Please approach the reference desk," said Ms. Waintraub, "to receive your official lPads."

"They're like iPads, but without the dot," added Mr. Lemoncello.

"Actually," stated the reference librarian, "they are tablet computers that will allow you to remotely search the Internet as well as the library's complete catalog and artifacts inventory."

"Now then," said Mr. Lemoncello, "let's all go to the lobby!" He shuffled sideways, raising a make-believe top hat and cane, while singing a song none of the contestants had ever heard before:

"Let's all go to the lobby;
let's all go to the lobby;
let's all go to the lobby
to watch you guys compete!"

Once in the lobby, Kyle saw a bright yellow lemon decal plastered to the floor.

"This lemon will be your starting square as well as your finish square, because I *love* lemon squares, even though a lemon is actually more of an oval," declared Mr. Lemoncello.

The security guards, Clarence and Clement, swung open the heavy, twelve-foot-wide, three-foot-thick circular front door, which came from the old Gold Dome Bank's vault. It was made of steel-clad concrete and weighed twenty tons.

With the door open, Kyle could see six Lemoncello Library bookmobiles parked at the curb. There were also six backpacks lined up on the sidewalk—three black bags with a lightbulb graphic silk-screened on the back, and three tomato-red bags with a blocky black "23" trimmed in white.

"That was Michael Jordan's number when he played with the Chicago Bulls," Kyle heard Angus whisper to Akimi.

"Today three teams will research the renowned inventor Thomas Alva Edison," said Mr. Lemoncello. "And three teams will investigate the legendary basketball great Michael 'Air' Jordan."

"So we're just supposed to race around town and find some random fact about Michael Jordan and Thomas Edison?" whined Andrew Peckleman, who'd never been the biggest fan of Mr. Lemoncello's games.

"Heavens, no. In those backpacks you will find a clue as well as snacks and beverages. Solve the clue and it will lead you to more clues. Solve your riddles and puzzles along the way until you find your fascinating factoid. The first two Edison teams and first two Jordan teams to return to the lemon square with the correct information will move on to the second round. Please note: To encourage independent thinking, no two teams will receive the exact same set of clues."

Diane Capriola raised her hand because Andrew was nudging her with his elbow. "Andrew wants to know what happens to the other two teams? The ones that come back with the answer *last*."

"I think we'd all like to know," said Andrew defensively.

Mr. Lemoncello smiled. "They lose. Because in every race ever run, in order for someone to win, someone else must lose."

16

"Okeydokey," said Mr. Lemoncello. "Since Abia and Kyle solved the Galileo rebus first, they get to go first. The other five teams will follow at ten-second intervals, based on the order you answered the icebreaker."

"Who do you want to grab?" Kyle asked Abia as he shook out his arms and limbered up his legs on the lemon-shaped decal.

"I have a slight preference for Edison," said Abia. "And you?"

"I'm good either way. I'll grab the Edison backpack and look inside it for a clue. You grab one of the bookmobiles."

"Why?"

"Because they wouldn't be parked out there if we weren't going to need them."

Abia nodded thoughtfully. "You make an excellent point, Kyle Keeley."

"Could you just call me Kyle?"

"Why?"

"Never mind."

"On your mark," said Mr. Lemoncello, "get set, Luigi, Lemon, cello, go!"

Abia and Kyle raced out the door and down the front steps.

Kyle grabbed one of the lightbulb backpacks while Abia stuck two fingers into her mouth and whistled a shrill blast at the bookmobile parked at the front of the line. Kyle had forgotten: Abia Sulayman was a big-city girl from Boston. She definitely knew how to hail a ride.

Kyle unzipped pockets on the book bag until he found a bright yellow envelope. It had to be the clue. He clutched it in one hand and the backpack in the other and hopped into the first bookmobile, which already had its engine running.

"You ready to roll, kids?" asked the driver, a college-aged girl named Jessica, according to the embroidery on her polo shirt.

"Not yet," said Kyle, tearing open the clue envelope.

"Why not?" asked Abia.

Kyle fumbled with the cello-shaped greeting card tucked inside the yellow envelope. "Because we won't know where we're supposed to go until we solve this riddle."

"Hurry, then!" said Abia, peering out the side window. "Akimi Hughes and Angus Harper have also picked up a lightbulb bag. Sierra Russell and Jamal Davis have gone for

Michael Jordan. Andrew Peckleman and Diane Capriola are taking Edison, too! And, if I remember correctly, the girl from Georgia is much better at solving riddles than you."

Thanks for reminding me, thought Kyle.

Heart racing, Kyle opened up the card and read the clue.

This place is crowded and dark,
So you can see stars during the day.
I rhyme with "in a park."
For popcorn and pop you'll pay.

"What is this 'in a park'?" asked Abia.

"Nothing. They're just nonsense words for the rhyme."

"So how are we to make sense of this if we have nothing but nonsense to work with?"

"It's a riddle," said Kyle.

"Oh," said the driver. "Is this Mr. Lemoncello's big new game for the holiday season? I heard he had something revolutionary coming down the pike."

"This is not it," said Abia, crossing her arms over her chest. "This is simply meaningless. . . ."

"Not really," said Kyle. "Where is it crowded and dark and you can see stars during the day?"

"A planetarium," said Abia.

"We don't have one of those," said Kyle. "But we have movie theaters!"

"So?"

"So you can see movie stars in a crowded, dark movie theater where you can also pay a ton of money for popcorn and pop. Driver?"

"Please, call me Jessica. 'Driver' sounds so chauffeur-ish."

" 'Chauffeurish' is not a word," said Abia.

"Should be."

"Fine," said Kyle. "Jessica—take us to the Alexandria-ville Cinemark movie theater."

The driver slipped the bookmobile into drive.

"Of course," said Abia, finally catching on, " 'Cinemark' rhymes with 'in a park'! Now drive like you stole this vehicle, Jessica!"

They zipped down Main Street and hung a sharp left turn on Maple.

Abia twisted around in her seat and looked out the rear window.

"The bookmobile ferrying Andrew Peckleman and Diane Capriola is following us. I told you Diane Capriola was a faster riddle solver than you, Kyle Keeley. We have lost our slight and insignificant lead."

Kyle sighed and slumped down in his seat.

Thanks for reminding me of that, too!

17

The theater marquee outside the art deco Cinemark movie theater in downtown Alexandriaville listed six different movie titles.

Five were big blockbusters. One Kyle had never heard of: *Another Clue for You*.

"Come on," said Kyle.

"Where are we going?" asked Abia.

"The box office. I want to see *Another Clue for You*."

"Ah, yes. I have heard that one is quite good. Well played, Kyle Keeley."

"Thanks."

They ran over to the ticket window.

"May I help the following guest?" asked the blue-haired lady inside the box office. Kyle noticed that she was wearing a little lemon-and-cello lapel pin.

"Mr. Lemoncello sent us!" said Kyle. "We'd like two tickets to *Another Clue for You*."

The lady thumped a button.

A tiny square of cardboard shot out of a metal slot in the ticket counter. The lady tore it off at its perforations and slid it through the half-moon window.

There was a miniature picture puzzle on the ticket stub.

"Enjoy your show. Next."

"Come on," said Kyle. "Let's go figure this out!"

They turned around. Andrew, Diane, Akimi, and Angus were all lined up behind them.

"We want to see the exact same movie," whined Andrew, nervously tapping his fingers on the counter.

"Good luck, you guys," said Akimi as Kyle and Abia hurried into the lobby to work their clue.

"Yeah," added Angus. "You're gonna need it!"

Akimi and Angus laughed and slapped each other high fives. They even woo-hooed.

Kyle couldn't let it bug him. He and Abia went over to a tall table near the concession stand and studied their clue.

"It's another pictogram!" said Kyle.

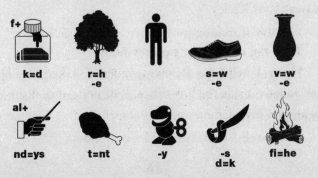

"Don't let the others see that!" whispered Abia.

"Don't worry. They're all getting different clues, remember?"

Kyle focused on the rebus. So did Abia.

Kyle figured it out first.

"Got it!" he said. "We need to 'find the man who was always meant to work here.'"

Kyle and Abia looked around the lobby. There was a guy tearing tickets. Two guys working behind the concession stand. An elderly man sweeping popcorn off the floor. Still another guy with a flashlight looped through his belt who looked like an usher.

All five of them wore the telltale lemon-and-cello lapel pins. So did all the women working in the movie theater.

"How do we find out which one of those men was always meant to work here?" asked Kyle.

"We could interview them," said Abia. "This is theoretically a game designed to test our research skills. The one-on-one interview is a time-honored investigatory technique."

"But it could take like an hour," said Kyle. "Maybe longer."

"Always searching for a shortcut, eh, Kyle Keeley?"

"Yes! Because this is a race!"

The guy working the broom shuffled by, chasing a half-popped kernel of corn that wouldn't stay in his long-handled dustpan.

"Very well," said Abia. "I have found one."

"What?"

"That senior citizen who just swept by. Did you notice his name tag?"

"No."

"He is Mark."

"So?"

"This is the Cinemark movie theater, is it not? Given Mr. Lemoncello's love of puns, clearly a man named Mark was always meant to work at a cinema named Cine-*mark*."

"Booyah!" exclaimed Kyle.

The two of them chased after the broom man, who had finally corralled the last pesky piece of popcorn.

"Excuse me, sir?" said Kyle. "Are you Cine-*mark*?"

The old man laughed. "Well, that's what Mr. Lemoncello always calls me because I know so much about movies."

"Um, do you know Thomas Edison?"

"I'm only seventy-two, son. Not a hundred and seventy-two."

"I know, but . . ."

"Ah, I'm just messing with you. Hang on."

He pulled a sheet of paper out of his pants pocket.

"Here we go. I'm supposed to say this to anybody who asks me about Edison." He cleared his throat. "Go to Murphy's Drugstore and grab what you might need if you were the star of the first copyrighted motion picture shot on an Edison Kinetoscope."

Kyle had no idea what the man was talking about. "We have to read Edison's horoscope?"

"We should return to our bookmobile," said Abia. "We can research Thomas Edison's contributions to the motion picture art form, including his creation known as the Kinetoscope."

"Sure," said Kyle, "we can do an Internet search on our tablet computers on the way to Murphy's."

"We can also consult the many books in our bookmobile. Knowing Mr. Lemoncello, I would not be surprised if several of them were from the 791.43 section."

"Which one is that, again?"

"Books dealing with the cinema."

"Right. I used to know that."

Abia could do it the old-fashioned way, with books, but Kyle would stick with a quick and speedy Google search.

Because the race always went to the swift!

18

Even though the Fabulous Fact-Finding Frenzy was under way, the Lemoncello Library was still open to the general public.

Frederick and David Krinkle had returned to Alexandriaville, this time to use one of the computers built into every reading desk under the rotunda.

"Here it is," said Frederick, clacking keys with one finger. "The Wikipedia entry I told you about."

"And you can change it?"

"Yes, David. That's what makes these things so wonderful. And if anybody cares to check, they will see that these edits were made from a computer here in Lemoncello's library."

He finished tapping in his entry. "There we are. A few fascinating facts that all the other contributors to this page somehow failed to mention."

David studied the computer screen. "Luigi Lemoncello was a high school dropout?"

"If it's on the Internet, it has to be true. Of course, dropping out of high school may have been a good move on Luigi's part because, as you will notice if you scroll down, he was kicked off his high school chess team for cheating."

"That was *you*, Frederick," said David. "You went to the bathroom during a tournament and consulted a cheat guide to plot your next move. The teacher in the adjoining stall caught you."

"Funny," said Frederick. "It seems Luigi did exactly the same thing."

The two brothers tittered.

"Our work here is done," said David. "It's time we checked in with our local research assistant."

"Yes," said Frederick. "Hopefully, she has found some information about the blockbuster game we will be announcing for the holidays—before the Imagination Factory announces it first!"

The two brothers packed up their things and headed into the lobby, with its ludicrous statue of Luigi standing on a lily pad spewing water out of his mouth like a broken drinking fountain.

"David! Frederick!" hollered the familiar voice of their number one nemesis.

He was standing near a lemon-shaped floor decal, holding a stopwatch.

"What brings you back here like a pair of bad pennies from heaven?"

"We wanted to see your new library," said David, his eyelid twitching. "It truly is marvelous. So generous of you to give up your valuable game-designing time for such a noble cause."

"Thank you, David. And what have you two been up to lately? Mass-producing cheap imitations of my extremely inventive games?"

"You're just jealous," snapped Frederick. "We outsold you in several markets last season."

"Two," said Mr. Lemoncello. "Two is a couple, not several. Two is not even a few."

"Well, just you wait for this year!" said Frederick, his face turning the color of a plum. "Your holiday line will be a complete and utter failure!"

All of a sudden Michael Jordan, wearing his Chicago Bulls uniform, strolled across the marble floor, casually dribbling a basketball.

"Th-th-that's Michael Jordan!" blurted Frederick.

"What's *he* doing here?" asked David.

"He isn't," said Mr. Lemoncello.

"What?"

"He's not here. He is, in truth, a hologram."

"Impossible."

"If I may quote Muhammad Ali," said Jordan, " 'Impossible is not a fact. It's an opinion.' "

Mr. Lemoncello beamed and bounced up on the heels

of his shoes. "So that's what I've been tinkering with lately. How about you boys?"

"We have several irons in the fire."

"Careful," said Mr. Lemoncello. "They might melt. And when they do, how will you press the wrinkles out of your stiffly starched shirts?"

Just then, four young people came bounding up the front steps of the library, dashed through the wide-open front door, and jumped on top of the lemon.

"We've got the answer!" they all shouted at the same time.

"Voice in the ceiling?" cried Mr. Lemoncello.

"According to floor pressure sensors," cooed a computerized voice, "both teams crossed the finish line at the same time."

"Very well," said Mr. Lemoncello, "Miguel and Pranav, Elliott and Katherine, kindly march over to the whiteboards conveniently located at opposite ends of the lobby and write down your fascinating fact about Mr. Jordan!"

The kids did as Mr. Lemoncello instructed. Katherine pulled out her small black book to make sure she remembered what she and her partner had decided to give as an answer.

The boys, Miguel and Pranav, couldn't decide who had the better penmanship. Finally, Miguel handed the dry-erase marker to Pranav.

"So," said David, "is this some sort of new game?"

"Oh, no," said Mr. Lemoncello. "This is the oldest

game in the book: thorough and proper research! We've just made it a little more fun. Because if something is fun, more of it gets done! By the way, do you two gentlemen know Miss Katherine Kelly?" He gestured toward the girl with long blond hair. "She hails from Kansas City, Missouri. I believe that's your hometown as well."

"Nope," said David. "Never met her."

"Come on, little brother," said Frederick. "We need to leave."

And they did. Fast.

19

"Victory goes to the swift!" declared Mr. Lemoncello. "Or in this case, all four of you swiftees!"

"I am very impressed," said the holographic Michael Jordan.

The two teams had followed their separate clue paths to arrive at the same answer: When he played in the NBA, for good luck Michael Jordan always wore blue-and-white University of North Carolina shorts under his red-and-black Chicago Bulls shorts.

"Mr. Jordan went to college at UNC, which he led to the NCAA championship in 1982," said Miguel.

"North Carolina's colors are blue and white," said Elliott. "Mr. Jordan thought the mesh marvels brought him luck, so he wore them like underpants when he turned pro!"

"Thanks for sharing that," said Jordan sort of sheepishly. "Any of you kids ever hear of TMI?"

"Our clues led us to Casey's Sports on Main Street," added Katherine, checking her notebook. "A clerk there named Shana told us about the North Carolina shorts."

"*Our* riddles took us to Atomic Athletic," explained Pranav. "We met a friendly clerk as well!"

"Proving," said Mr. Lemoncello, "that there is always more than one way to bake a cake, peel an orange, shine a penny, or find an answer about orange cakes with penny candy on top!"

"And you can take *that* to the hoop!" said Michael Jordan as a basketball net appeared on the keystone of the arch leading into the rotunda. Jordan took two giant strides as an arena full of cheering fans and a play-by-play announcer's excited voice roared out of the ceiling speakers.

"Uh-oh, catch him if you can. There goes Jordan! Flying through the air! He is airborne!"

The basketball legend leapt, floated in midair, and, just before he was about to dunk it, tossed the holographic ball over his shoulder to Mr. Lemoncello, who took a jump shot and sent the make-believe ball flying back through the make-believe net.

A buzzer sounded.

"Oh, my goodness!" cried the announcer. "What a play. Luigi Lemoncello from downtown at the buzzer with an assist from Air Jordan!"

Miguel, Pranav, Katherine, and Elliott clapped furiously as Michael Jordan smiled, waved, and disappeared—all while floating six feet off the ground.

"This Nonfictionator is amazing!" declared Miguel. "It's the coolest thing you've ever invented, sir!"

"So far, Miguel," said Mr. Lemoncello with a sly twinkle in his eye. "So far!"

That's when Sierra and Jamal, the third team in the Michael Jordan leg of the quest, came strolling up the front steps of the library toting canvas book bags. Both were reading the same book as they stepped through the circular front door.

"It reminds me most of *The Westing Game*," said Sierra.

"Really?" said Jamal. "I find it to be a cross between *Charlie and the Chocolate Factory, The Gollywhopper Games,* and *The Puzzling World of Winston Breen.*"

"Still, it's quite good," said Sierra.

"Oh, yes," said Jamal. "I couldn't put it down. Neither could my younger brother."

They were so absorbed in their book talk they didn't see the four other players and Mr. Lemoncello eagerly awaiting their arrival. They didn't even bother to step on the big lemon.

Finally, Mr. Lemoncello broke their bookish trance.

"Sooooo," he said, "did you two find a fascinating fact for us?"

"No," said Sierra. "Sorry."

"Book Culture, the store on Main Street, was having a huge buy-one, get-one-free sale," explained Jamal.

"We couldn't resist," said Sierra. She saw the four other data dashers grinning widely. "Are we late?"

"Yes, Sierra," said Mr. Lemoncello, " 'Late' would be the right word, according to Roget and his thesaurus."

"Oh, well," said Jamal. "Now we can go hang out in the fiction section and ride the hover ladders. Sierra was telling me about this awesome poetry book by Kwame Alexander."

"It's sort of about basketball," said Sierra. "That's what Michael Jordan played, right?"

Mr. Lemoncello just smiled. "Enjoy your time in the library, Sierra and Jamal. Find a good book and get lost in it."

"Oh, we will," said Sierra.

"Definitely," said Jamal.

"We'll see you two at the gala!" Mr. Lemoncello turned to the two winning teams. "As for the rest of you? Let's hit the Book Nook Café and grab some lunch. We'll start the second leg of our Fabulous Fact-Finding Frenzy tomorrow morning. Hmm. The second leg reminds me of my little brother Massimo. At Thanksgiving dinner, he always ate both drumsticks."

Mr. Lemoncello led the way back into the rotunda.

Over at the far wall, Sierra and Jamal floated up the three-story-tall fiction bookcase on a pair of hover ladders. The gliding platforms—with safety braces, handrails, and book baskets—used magnetic levitation technology to take library patrons up to the novel they were searching for (unless you used the browse button, of course—then you just flitted back and forth until something caught your eye).

Michael Jordan was browsing the fiction wall, too.

But he didn't need a hover ladder to levitate. He could just leap up to snag a book as if it were a rebound coming off the backboard.

Of course, since he was a hologram, he couldn't actually *grab* a real book.

But he sure looked awesome trying!

20

As the lumbering bookmobile raced across town, Kyle and Abia sat in the back doing their independent research projects.

Kyle quickly Googled "Thomas Edison's first movie."

Abia consulted a stack of books from the 791.43 section of the library that were conveniently shelved in the back of the bookmobile.

"These cinema books are not in this vehicle by accident, Kyle Keeley," she said.

"Maybe not," said Kyle, balancing his lPad on his lap. "But we don't need 'em. Google just told me what we needed to know: The first silent movie, produced in 1903, was Thomas Edison's *The Great Train Robbery*. Plot's pretty basic. Four bandits rob a train. Posse chases them. Shootout. Bad guys bite the dust. The end."

"If that is the correct answer, why did the third clue send us to a drugstore?" asked Abia.

"Because Murphy's sells all sorts of stuff—including toys. They have these bags filled with plastic cowboys. That's where we'll find our fascinating fact about Edison."

"I respectfully disagree," said Abia. "It is too easy an answer. We need to dig deeper."

"Fine. Dig all you want. They sell garden tools at Murphy's, too. Me? I'm heading for the toy bin and digging for a bag filled with tiny plastic cowboys!"

When they reached Murphy's Drugstore, neither of the other two Edison teams was there.

"Guess their clues sent them somewhere else," remarked Kyle as he checked out the store. "The toys are back this way."

"Have fun," said Abia. "I will be searching in the cold-remedy section."

"Why?"

"Because, Kyle Keeley, I did a more thorough search of the data than you did."

"Right. Because I got the answer on the first try. Boom! Why don't you just wait here and I'll go grab our next clue?"

"No thank you."

"Suit yourself."

They took off in opposite directions.

Kyle went to the toy department and found a bin of

clear plastic bags stuffed with multicolored, five-inch-tall plastic cowboys.

"Right out of *The Great Train Robbery*!" he said with a grin.

Kyle started examining the bags. Each one had two dozen cowboy figures striking maybe five different poses. There were also a couple corral fences in the bags—but no bright yellow clue cards.

"Are you finished playing with your cowboys, Kyle Keeley?"

He whipped around. Abia was in the toy aisle, holding a tissue box decorated with yellow lemons and brown cellos.

"What's that?" asked Kyle.

"Our next clue. *The Great Train Robbery* may have been the first *silent film* produced by Thomas Edison, but the first copyrighted motion picture shot on an Edison Kinetoscope—which, by the way, is what the clue specifically asked us to identify—was a five-second-long, black-and-white filmstrip of one of Mr. Edison's assistants, a gentleman named Fred Ott, sneezing. He might need this."

She wiggled the Kleenex box.

"All that was in those books in the back of the bookmobile?" asked Kyle.

"All except the tissue. I figured out that part by attempting to think in the same manner that you often employ when deciphering one of Mr. Lemoncello's riddles."

"So I helped you find the answer, right?"

"Oh, yes," she said sarcastically. "You helped a great deal."

"I was kidding. You get all the credit on this one. Was there anything in the box?"

"A final riddle: 'Race back to the library, and when you know the answer, tell Mr. Lemoncello who invented the lightbulb.'"

"Easy!" said Kyle. "Thomas Edison."

"Too easy," said Abia. "The first answer is not always the best answer. Besides, there is a number printed at the bottom of the clue card: 621.32097309034."

"Okay," said Kyle. "That's definitely a Dewey decimal number."

"Correct."

"Come on. We can use our lPads to do a catalog search on the ride back to the library."

"I have already done one," said Abia as they hit the sidewalk. "It is a book on Thomas Edison."

"Which is going to tell us that he's the guy who invented the lightbulb!"

"Perhaps. But if that is the case, why does this clue encourage us to do further research?"

"Because someone's trying to slow us down."

They climbed into the bookmobile.

"We can't afford to waste time," said Kyle. "Come on, this is one we know the answer to!"

"Do we?" asked Abia. "Just like we knew a bag of plastic cowboys was the answer?"

She had him there.

"Fine," said Kyle. "We'll go read another book, even though everybody in third grade knows that Thomas Edison invented the lightbulb."

They rode back to the library in silence.

When they entered the lobby, they saw Andrew Peckleman and Diane Capriola standing on the lemon square, facing Mr. Lemoncello.

"Do not stop, Kyle Keeley," said Abia. "Upstairs. The six hundreds room."

"Upstairs," muttered Kyle, because he'd agreed to play this one Abia's way. "The six hundreds room."

But as they dashed up the curving staircases from the lobby to the second floor, Kyle could hear Andrew and Diane loudly proclaiming their answer.

"Thomas Edison invented the lightbulb!" whined Andrew. "Duh!"

"Everybody knows that," added Diane.

Yeah, thought Kyle. *Everybody except Abia Sulayman.*

21

"Here it is," announced Abia, reaching for the book with 621.32097309034 on its spine. *"The Age of Edison: Electric Light and the Invention of Modern America* by Ernest Freeberg."

"Okay, it took like half an hour just to read the title!" said Kyle, who was totally exasperated with his partner.

Meanwhile, Abia was dutifully checking the index, flipping through pages, and examining the dense text.

"We need to hurry up. Andrew and Diane already gave the right answer. Akimi and Angus are probably down there right now doing the same thing. We're gonna lose!"

"If Akimi and Angus give the same answer that Andrew and Diane just gave, then they, too, will have answered incorrectly."

She tapped a passage.

Kyle scanned it.

According to the book, Edison was not the lone genius inventor of the lightbulb. He was in a very competitive race, where he borrowed—some said stole—ideas from other inventors who were also working on an incandescent bulb.

"So," said Kyle, "what's the answer? Who invented the lightbulb?"

"Many different individuals," said Abia. "Including British scientists Humphrey Davy and Warren De la Rue, plus the Canadian team of Woodward and Evans, who sold their patent for an electric lightbulb to Thomas Alva Edison."

"That's our answer?" asked Kyle. "All sorts of people?"

"Yes!" said Abia.

"Fine," said Kyle. "What've we got to lose? Except, you know, the *whole entire game!*"

They hurried around the second-floor balcony to the grand staircase sweeping down to the lobby, where they saw Akimi and Angus standing on the lemon square doing an end zone victory dance.

Mr. Lemoncello stood beside a hologram of a bald man in a bow tie wearing an old-fashioned three-piece wool suit. A watch chain dangled between his vest pockets. Kyle figured the Nonfictionator had just cooked up Thomas Alva Edison.

But Mr. Edison didn't look too happy. His head was sort of hanging low.

"Are we too late?" asked Kyle as he and Abia descended the steps.

"No," said Mr. Lemoncello. "Fortunately, just like the milk, Akimi and Angus had the correct answer. Andrew and Diane, unfortunately, did not."

Kyle looked at Abia. Her grin was extremely wide.

"Go on," he told her. "Give our team answer."

"Thank you, Kyle Keeley. It shall be my pleasure. Our answer is 'A lot of different scientists and inventors contributed to the invention of the electric lightbulb.' "

"You are correct," said Mr. Lemoncello. "Therefore, Abia and Kyle will join Akimi and Angus and move on to the next leg of the competition, where the four of you will go up against Elliott and Katherine, Miguel and Pranav—the winners for the Michael Jordan exhibit. Congratulicitations!"

"Way to go, Kyle," said Akimi.

"It was all Abia on this one," said Kyle.

"Wait a second," wailed Edison. "I am the Wizard of Menlo Park! I am a genius!"

"Indeed you are, sir," said Abia respectfully. "But, if I may be so bold, your true genius was your ability to coordinate all the various research being done by others around the incandescent lightbulb to create a mass-producible result."

Edison turned to Lemoncello. "Does everybody in the world need to know this? I like the story they tell kids in grade school better. I did it all by myself."

"Sorry, Tom," said Mr. Lemoncello. "At the Lemoncello Library, we value the truth more than myths."

"What about all those Percy Jackson books you have?" fumed Edison. "Those are myths!"

"And they are correctly shelved as fiction."

"You also kind of stole a few ideas," Akimi said to Edison. "Like from those two Canadian guys."

"I did not steal anything," said Edison. "I bought their patents. Paying for knowledge is an acceptable form of research and development."

"Tell me, Thomas," said Mr. Lemoncello, "did you ever hire a fellow named Benjamin Bean to do 'research and development' for you?"

"Bean? Never heard of him," said Edison. "Now, if you will excuse me, I must go invent the talking doll!"

With that, Thomas Edison vanished.

22

Up bright and early the next day, Kyle hurried to the library for the second leg of the amazing research race.

He was happy to be moving on to the next round and felt bad for the teams that didn't make it through. It could've been him—especially if he hadn't listened to Abia.

Four bookmobiles were lined up at the curb near the library's front entrance. Four fresh backpacks waited on the sidewalk.

Two of them had the silhouette of a pretty cool-looking biplane. Two had "Dwell in Possibility" written in frilly script letters.

"That's for Emily Dickinson, right?" he whispered to Abia.

"Correct. She was the poet who wrote 'I dwell in Possibility, A fairer House than Prose, More numerous of Windows, Superior—for Doors—'"

"So, she was also into architecture?"

Abia looked at Kyle. "Perhaps we should go for the biplane and the Wright brothers?"

"Definitely," said Kyle.

The three other teams were also eyeballing the backpacks and whispering to each other, plotting their strategies.

The red door leading from the lobby into the control room swung open, and out stepped Mr. Lemoncello. He was dressed like a big bird. Not *the* Big Bird—some kind of Dr. Seuss creature with gangly legs, an odd beak, and two weird tail feathers.

"An *egg*ceptionally good morning to you all! Today's competition will be all about flying and poetic flights of fancy as you research the Wright brothers and Emily Dickinson. To determine the order of your book bag grab, kindly identify which poetic bird I am currently portraying."

He preened and yawned and looked at his watch like he was bored.

Seven of the contestants looked like they were confused.

But not Kyle. Dr. Seuss was his favorite. He loved when his parents used to read Seuss stories to him at bedtime.

"If you look at your lPads," Mr. Lemoncello continued, "you will notice that a Who Am I? game has just popped out."

Kyle heard eight *DA-DING!*s.

"When you know the answer, enter it! On your mark, get set, Lemon, cello, go!"

Everyone stood in the lobby, staring blankly at their tablet computers.

"Do you know this?" asked Abia.

"I think so. The yawn was a hint. . . ."

"Then type it in!"

Kyle started tapping the glass pad.

Mr. Lemoncello started squawking poetry. "You've nothing to do, and I do need a rest."

Katherine Kelly grabbed the lPad from Elliott Schilpp. Kyle could tell: She knew the answer, too!

Mr. Lemoncello completed the stanza: "Would you like to sit on the egg in my nest?"

Kyle hit send. Miguel and Akimi, who'd finally figured out what Seuss book Mr. Lemoncello was quoting, typed in answers for their teams.

Mr. Lemoncello's sleek black wristwatch (which looked bizarre on his feathered arm) blared like a tiny tin trumpet. He held it to his ear.

"What? Hello? Who are you?"

He squinted and read what must've been written in very small Whoville-sized type on the watch's screen.

"Aha! You've all guessed correctly. I am, indeed, currently costumed as Mayzie, the lazy bird from *Horton Hatches the Egg*. The team of Kyle and Abia came in first, Katherine and Elliott second, Miguel and Pranav third, Akimi and Angus fourth—but only by an *eggs*-traordinarily slim margin. You will now, once again, depart in ten-second intervals. Good luck. And happy hunting!"

Mr. Lemoncello raised his arm. The tiny Whoville trumpet in his wristwatch blared a bugle call.

"Go!" he shouted.

Kyle and Abia dashed out the door, down the steps, and onto the sidewalk, where they grabbed one of the Wright brothers backpacks.

"First bookmobile!" shouted Abia. "Go!"

They jumped into the back of the vehicle.

"Where to?" asked the driver, whose name was Mad Dog. Seriously. It was stitched over his pocket.

"Hang on," said Kyle.

He unzipped the front pocket of the backpack.

"We've got another riddle," he reported.

"What does it say?" asked Abia.

Kyle read the yellow note card:

To win this round, you might need to be
what a North Carolina license plate tells you to be.

"Quick," said Abia. "Now is the time for Googling. What is the slogan on a North Carolina license plate?"

They both tapped in the search words "North Carolina license plate slogan."

"First in flight!" said Abia, who'd done an image search. "It depicts the Wright brothers' biplane."

"So to win, we need to be the 'first in flight.'"

"Where is the nearest airport?"

"Mad Dog!" shouted Kyle. "Take us to Wood County Regional!"

"Do you have your permission slips?" asked the driver.

"Yes!" screamed Kyle and Abia. "Hurry!"

Mad Dog slammed the bookmobile into gear and grabbed a radio microphone with a coiled cord.

"This is Bookmobile One," he said to whoever was on the receiving end. "We are on the way to the airport."

"Very good," said Mr. Lemoncello through the bookmobile's speakers. "Kindly inform your passengers that there are two flights departing to North Carolina at this hour. Whoever finds it first gets to fly in my corporate jet."

"Booyah!" said Kyle.

"Katherine and Elliott are right behind us," reported Abia. "They must've figured out the riddle, too."

"The second vehicle to the airstrip," continued Mr. Lemoncello, "will have a somewhat slower flight in my recently retired prop plane."

"Punch it, sir!" Abia shouted at the driver.

The bookmobile lurched forward.

Kyle was glad they'd grabbed the first bookmobile at the curb.

When you were in a mad dash to the airport, it was always good to have a driver named Mad Dog!

23

One second after Mad Dog brought the bookmobile to a tire-squealing stop, Kyle and Abia hopped out the sliding side door, grabbed their backpack, and dashed for the hangars where the private planes were parked.

"Whoa, hold up there, kids," said a burly security guard, raising her hand and blocking the gate in a chainlink fence topped with coils of barbed wire. "This is a restricted area."

"Mr. Lemoncello sent us!" said Kyle breathlessly.

"We are Abia Sulayman and Kyle Keeley."

The guard flipped through sheets of paper on her clipboard. "Sulayman, Sulayman, Sulay, Man . . ."

"We're kind of in a hurry," said Kyle.

"Most folks at an airport are. Rush, rush, rush. No one wants to slow down and smell the exhaust fumes anymore."

The guard flicked back to the first page on her clipboard. "Sulayman . . ."

Kyle heard tires squeal, a door slide open and then slam shut.

Katherine and Elliott's bookmobile had just skidded to a stop behind Kyle and Abia's.

"Run!" shouted their driver. It was Jessica, the driver Kyle and Abia had for the first leg of the race.

"Grab the backpack!" cried Elliott.

"You don't have time!" said the driver. "Hurry! You'll lose the jet!"

Kyle's heart raced faster than Mad Dog drove as Katherine and Elliott sprinted toward the gate.

"Ma'am?" he said to the security guard. "We really need to—"

The phone clipped to the guard's belt buzzed. "Here we are. The boss just texted over your names. Keeley and Sulayman, you are good to go." She stepped away from the gate. "Have a nice flight."

"Run!" shouted Kyle.

"Fast!" Abia shouted back.

They only had a twenty-yard lead on the competition, who barely had to break stride when they reached the guard at the gate because now she had a list of approved names!

There were several aluminum-sided buildings at the far end of the airfield. None of them were marked with lemons, cellos, or Imagination Factory logos.

"Which hangar is Mr. Lemoncello's?" Abia asked Kyle as they continued their sprint.

"Don't know," said Kyle between gasps for air. "But I bet it's the biggest one."

"Let us play your hunch!"

Abia and Kyle darted on a diagonal. Now Katherine and Elliott were only *fifteen* yards behind them.

"They're following us!" shouted Abia.

"Because they think we know where we're going!" said Kyle.

He grabbed the door. Swung it open.

There were six planes parked inside the hangar. Three were corporate jets. Three were propeller planes. All were painted in shades of yellow. One of the jets was sculpted with a slight curve along its body so it resembled a banana with wings. There were also bananas decorating the wingtips.

"That's his jet!" Kyle told Abia. They started running for it. "Mr. Lemoncello's biggest hit last year was his burp-squeaking banana shoes!"

"How do you know this?"

"I'm a huge fan!"

They made it to the jet ten seconds before Katherine and Elliott.

The door opened and a staircase eased down.

"Welcome aboard, Kyle and Abia," said the flight attendant at the top of the stairs. "Do you have your permission slips?"

"Yes!" said Kyle and Abia, gasping for breath.

"Then Mr. Lemoncello's private jet is all yours." She looked to Katherine and Elliott. "You two will be flying to North Carolina in Mr. Lemoncello's recently retired Lemon Drop Prop." Then she smiled and waved. "Buh-bye, now. Have a good day. Buh-bye."

Katherine and Elliott slumped off toward the propeller plane.

Feeling triumphant, Kyle and Abia scampered up the steps to the jet's door.

The interior of Mr. Lemoncello's private plane was unbelievably amazing. There were four Barcalounger-type recliner chairs facing one another around a circular game table. Each of the chairs had its own computer on a swivel that you could tuck away into the armrest. The jet was decorated with so many bright colors, it was sort of like flying inside a jumbo-sized crayon box.

"There is a hot tub in the lavatory," said the flight attendant. "If you need towels or bathing suits, you will find them in the changing room just off the gymnasium with the stationary bikes."

"Will we have time to take a dip?" asked Kyle.

"Probably not. It's just a short hop to North Carolina. But please enjoy all the features of our in-flight entertainment system."

She gestured toward the bulkhead wall. It was a giant flat-screen TV where you could watch movies and satellite TV or play Mr. Lemoncello's latest video games.

"There is also a Goofitacious Gooseball table in the game cabin, which, as you may know, is a lot like foosball, but the players are shaped like geese and the ball like a goose egg, so it wobbles unpredictably when you whack it."

Kyle and Abia sniffed the delicious scents wafting through the cabin and followed the aroma into the galley, where a chef in a tall paper hat was pulling fresh-baked chocolate chip cookies out of an oven.

"Today's in-flight meal service offers a choice," the chef announced. "Chicago-style hot dogs. Or, from our halal menu, chicken and falafel over rice with white sauce and pita bread."

"The chicken, please," said Abia.

"Me too," said Kyle. "And the hot dog. And some of those cookies. I'm kind of hungry."

"This is the captain speaking," said a voice from the cabin's overhead speakers. "We are number one for take-off. Flight attendants, prepare the cabin for departure."

Kyle and Abia plopped into their plush recliners and strapped on their seat belts.

"We should probably skip all the fun stuff and do Wright brothers research instead, huh?" said Kyle.

Abia nodded. "Pre-research might help us identify the fact we'll need to find when we land in North Carolina."

"Good." Kyle settled into his seat. "I want to win this thing!"

"As do I."

111

The jet gently lifted off.

Abia turned to Kyle. "We make quite a formidable team."

"Yep. We sure do!"

Then they actually leaned in and slapped each other a high five.

24

"You folks are now officially ahead of the other team by thirty minutes," said the pilot when the banana jet landed at First Flight Airport in Kill Devil Hills, North Carolina. "Outside, to your south and east, you will find the Wright Brothers National Memorial and Museum."

"Thank you, sir!" said Abia.

"You're welcome, ma'am."

"And thanks for the food and stuff," said Kyle, who had eaten the halal meal, the hot dog, and maybe six of those chocolate chip cookies. "Will there be more snacks on the way back?"

"Roger that," said the pilot. "And they will be all yours—provided, of course, you two are the first team planeside with the fascinating fact Mr. L is looking for."

"You mean the race for the jet is still on?" said Abia,

burping up a little of the spicy white sauce from her chicken and rice.

"Affirmative. With Mr. Lemoncello, no race is ever over until it is over, ma'am. Enjoy your thirty-minute head start."

He saluted.

Kyle and Abia dashed down the staircase. They could smell salt water in the air because the ocean was just on the other side of the sand dunes. But neither one of them knew what they were looking for. Some sort of fascinating fact? It could be anything!

"Look," said Kyle. "Over there. Four weird bikes."

Outside the small terminal, four bicycles with giant front tires but tiny back tires were propped up on bike stands.

"How does one even climb up into the seat?" said Abia.

"Very carefully," said Kyle.

There was a sign planted in the ground near the antique bikes that let them know they were on the right track.

> This is what bicycles looked like before
> the Wright brothers came along.
> Use them to fly to where
> frozen figures stand in a throng.

"According to the research I did on the plane," said Abia, "the style of bicycle we know today was, more or less, invented by the Wright brothers in Ohio."

She and Kyle hauled themselves up to the tiny seats above the giant front wheels of the old-fashioned bikes.

"Now we need to find the statues," said Kyle.

"Statues? Why? What are you talking about?"

"Frozen figures. Those have to be statues."

"There!" said Abia, wobbling on her lofty perch. "Do you see it?"

"Yes!"

In a flat area below a stone monument on a sandy knoll, Kyle could see several bronze figures chasing after a replica of the Wright brothers' first-flight biplane. One of the figures was manning a camera on a tripod. One was running alongside the plane. Four were cheering the plane and pilot on, clumped together in a throng.

"The man with the camera is most likely John T. Daniels," said Abia.

"The guy who snapped the photo of the famous first flight," added Kyle, because he'd actually done some research on the flight from Ohio.

The teammates pedaled around the looped drive, teetering on their ridiculously high bicycle seats. As they drew near to the statues, they hopped the curb and bumped across dune grass to the edge of the sculpture garden.

"Dismount!" hollered Kyle, trying his best to keep his balance on what felt like a unicycle with one not-very-helpful training wheel.

"How?" cried Abia.

"Tip sideways, close your eyes, and hope for soft sand!"

115

They tumbled to the ground. It wasn't pretty.

"Are you okay?" Kyle asked.

"Yes. I have sand in my shoes, but I am otherwise fine."

"Good," said Kyle, running up to the bronze biplane. "That's Orville lying down and flying the thing," he said.

"And Wilbur running alongside the wingtip," said Abia.

"So what fact are we supposed to find?" said Kyle, looking around.

"There!" said Abia. "That statue of the man wearing the military cap. I see something yellow in each of his hands!"

Kyle and Abia dashed over to the statue. Bright yellow envelopes were sticky-taped to both of his bronze palms.

"Limit one clue per team, please" was printed on the front.

"Take the one on the right," suggested Abia.

Kyle grabbed it and tore the envelope open.

Here's a fact that's fun and not a bore:
Count the adults and you'll find four.
Now tell us more about Johnny Moore.

"Whaaa?" said Kyle.

"They might be able to help us inside the museum," said Abia, pointing to a small building several hundred yards away.

Overhead, Kyle heard the drone of an approaching aircraft.

"It sounds like a prop plane!" he said. "It's Katherine and Elliott!"

"Back on our bikes," said Abia. "Quickly."

It took about five minutes and a dozen tries—because the weird bikes with the ginormous front wheels weren't propped up in brackets anymore—but, just as Katherine and Elliott's plane landed, Kyle and Abia were back in their saddles and pumping pedals frantically.

Fortunately, when they reached the museum, there was another bike rack with four fairly normal-looking bikes. A yellow Lemoncello sign was attached to the end of the stand:

> You've made progress and, thanks to the
> Wright brothers, so did bicycles.
> Use one of these to travel back to
> the airfield and your flight home to Ohio.

Inside the museum, they found a National Parks tour guide named Rachel. She was wearing a lemon-and-cello pin on her brown park uniform shirt. That had to mean she was in on the game!

"Excuse me," said Kyle. "Can you please tell us about Johnny Moore?"

"Certainly," said Rachel. "Johnny Moore was a boy, a

little older than you two, who just happened to be walking along the beach on December seventeenth, 1903. He heard a commotion. Curious, he went to investigate and became the youngest witness to the Wright brothers' first flight."

"Bingo!" said Kyle.

"Excuse me?" said the nice park lady.

"This is our fascinating fact," added Abia. "Thank you, Rachel!"

Kyle and Abia bolted out of the museum, hopped on one of the normal bikes, sped back to the airstrip, and climbed into the banana jet just as Katherine and Elliott were wobbling their way on bikes from their plane to the statues.

"Woo-hoo!" shouted Kyle.

"Woo-hoo, indeed," said Abia.

The jet taxied to the runway and took off.

This time, the two teammates knocked knuckles.

25

Deplaning in Ohio, Kyle and Abia saw the two book-mobiles waiting in the airport parking lot.

Jessica, their driver from the first leg of the competition, was sitting in the back of her vehicle, zipping up the backpack Katherine and Elliott had dumped in their scramble to race to Mr. Lemoncello's jet first.

Jessica saw Kyle watching her.

"They left their sandwiches," she said with a smile. "And I'm starving!"

"Well, you better save them a few crumbs," said Kyle, still feeling kind of cocky. "I don't think their prop plane came equipped with a chef and gourmet meals. They were probably lucky to score one of those little peanut pouches and a watered-down pop!"

"Perhaps we should've saved them some of our freshly baked chocolate chip cookies," said Abia.

Then she and Kyle looked at each other.

"Naaaah," they said together.

Laughing, they climbed into their bookmobile.

"Back to the library, Mad Dog," said Kyle. "And I think you can take your time. Those other guys are probably somewhere over North Carolina!"

Kyle and Abia climbed up the steps of the library and stepped through the bank vault door. Mr. Lemoncello was standing with Mr. Raymo, the chief imagineer, and two turn-of-the-century gentlemen in high-collared shirts, tweed suits, and bowler hats.

"Hiya, Orville and Wilbur," said Kyle. "You guys look just like your statues."

"But not nearly as bronzed," added Abia, who, believe it or not, was actually cracking a joke. "Perhaps you need to work on your suntans."

"We can adjust that," said Mr. Raymo, tapping his tablet computer.

"She's joking," said Kyle. "Right?"

"Indeed," Abia said with a slight smile. "I fear it comes from spending too much time with you, Kyle Keeley."

Kyle grinned.

"Congratulicitations," said Mr. Lemoncello. "You two are the first team to return from the Outer Banks of North Carolina to the inner lobby of what used to be a bank in Ohio. Did you find your fascinating fact?"

"Indeed we did, sir," said Abia.

"Johnny Moore was just a kid whose curiosity made him part of history," said Kyle.

"He was the youngest of the five witnesses to the Wright brothers' first flight on that cold and blustery December day in 1903."

"It *was* rather nippy that morning," said Wilbur.

"And I was the one lying down on the plane, manning the controls," added Orville. "So I had to contend with the wind-chill factor as well."

"For twelve seconds," said Wilbur, rolling his eyes at his brother.

"Fine. Next time you do it."

"Boys?" said Mr. Lemoncello. "Don't make Mr. Raymo dial up your mother on his Nonfictionator." He turned to Kyle and Abia. "Well done. You two will be moving on to the final round. Your opponents, Elliott Schilpp and Katherine Kelly, will not."

"Who won the Emily Dickinson race?" asked Kyle.

"We did," said Akimi, strolling into the lobby with her partner, Angus.

"But they only beat us by like ten seconds," said Miguel as he and his partner, Pranav, joined the others in the lobby.

"If I may inquire," said Abia, "what was the fascinating fact you four discovered about Emily Dickinson?"

"We'll show you!" declared Mr. Lemoncello. "Mr. Raymo, if you please?"

"Certainly, sir." He started tapping on his tablet.

Orville and Wilbur Wright disappeared.

A frail young woman wearing a black dress with puffy shoulders faded into view. Her dark hair was pulled back from her pale face into a tight bun.

"Most of my poems," said the holographic Emily Dickinson, "employed what is known as the common meter."

"We studied that in school," said Kyle. "A meter is like six-tenths of a mile. . . ."

"In poetry," said Dickinson, " 'meter' refers to the pattern of beats."

"Her poems are mostly four beats followed by three," explained Miguel.

"So," added Angus, "you can sing 'em to the tune of 'The Yellow Rose of Texas.' "

"Or," said Pranav, "as we recently learned in our research quest, to the tune of the theme song from Mr. Lemoncello's favorite boyhood television show, *Gilligan's Island*."

"*Gilligan's Island*? What's it about?" asked Kyle.

"Why, it's a rollicking tale of seven castaways stranded on a desert island!" said Mr. Lemoncello. He started singing the theme song (slightly off-key): *"Just sit right back and you'll hear a tale, a tale of a fateful trip . . ."*

"I think Miss Dickinson's poetry might sound better," said Miguel. "Seriously. I do."

"Very well, Miguel," said Mr. Lemoncello. "Emily, if you please?"

The flickering Emily Dickinson recited the first stanza of one of her most famous poems to the tune of the *Gilligan's Island* theme song:

> "Because I could not stop for Death,
> He kindly stopped for me;
> The carriage held but just ourselves
> And Immortality."

Everyone in the lobby applauded wildly.

"And so," said Mr. Lemoncello after Emily Dickinson had disappeared, "we are down to our final two teams! Kyle and Abia versus Akimi and Angus. Tomorrow we will begin the final leg of the Fabulous Fact-Finding Frenzy. After that, one team, our most fabulous and frenzied fact finders, will be declared the winners and go on a grand North American library tour, where they will be hailed as research heroes and—"

"And take home the first copies of that new floating emoji game, right?" said Kyle.

"Right. You took the words out of my mouth. But don't worry, I gargled this morning. The other team? Well, like today's runners-up, you will receive lovely parting gifts including a lifetime supply of those Ohio confectionery treats known as buckeyes—chocolate-dipped peanut butter balls!"

The consolation prize actually sounded pretty good to Kyle, because he definitely loved Ohio's famous buckeye candies.

But as anybody could tell you, he loved winning even more.

26

"Ready, racers?" asked Mr. Lemoncello as the two remaining teams crowded each other on the lemon square in the library lobby first thing the next morning.

This was it, thought Kyle. The final race. Akimi and Angus versus Kyle and Abia. There was no tomorrow. Well, there was, but it was just a date on the calendar. Whoever won this one would win everything!

"Ready," said Kyle and Abia.

"Ready," said Angus, crouching down in a way that sort of shoved Kyle sideways.

"Careful there, Mr. Harper," said the hologram of Abraham Lincoln, who stood beside Mr. Lemoncello. Both of them were wearing tailcoats and stovepipe hats. "A house divided against itself cannot stand. Neither can a runner nudged in an unsportsmanlike manner."

"Sorry," said Angus. "Just eager to win."

"Oh," said Lincoln, "if only you had been one of my generals at the start of the Civil War . . ."

The eight other data dashers were assembled in the lobby to cheer on the final four contestants.

"Hurry up and win, somebody!" shouted Elliott. "There's a humongous Lincoln Log victory cake in the Book Nook Café! With buttercream frosting!"

"And lemon meringue pie," added Katherine.

Mr. Lemoncello gestured toward the open bank vault door.

"Since we are now down to our final two exhibits, Abraham Lincoln and *moi*, Luigi L. Lemoncello, we're shaking things up for this final leg of the great library race. You will notice that we have placed *four* backpacks on the sidewalk in front of two bookmobiles and four bicycles. The two yellow backpacks will take you on a knowledge quest into my own personal past. The two copper-colored bags with Mr. Lincoln's portrait on the back will lead you off, via the banana jet, to Columbus, Ohio, where Mr. Lincoln once gave a speech in 1859."

"Only fifty people came to hear me speak," said Lincoln with a sad sigh. "But, like I once said, you have to do your own growing no matter how tall your grandfather was."

"Well put, Mr. President!" exclaimed Mr. Lemoncello. "My most famous quote is 'My best friend is the man who'll get me a book I ain't read.' "

"I believe I said that one, too," said Lincoln.

"I know. But I just love quoting you." He turned to the two teams. "Researchers, you have a choice. Both teams can go for the Lincoln fact or both can go for the Lemoncello fact. Then again, one team could go for Lincoln, the other for Lemoncello. Or vice versa. Or the opposite of vice versa, which I believe is virtue versa! It's totally up to you. But remember, the last team back is a pair of rotten eggs."

Kyle looked at Abia. "Lemoncello?" he mouthed.

She nodded.

Next to them, Akimi and Angus were mouthing the same thing.

"All right, teams, are you ready?" Mr. Lemoncello raised his arm. "On your mark, get set, Lemon, cello, go!"

The four remaining contestants dashed for the circular doorway. There was a bit of a traffic jam at first, but they all finally worked themselves free of the arm-elbow-leg tangle and raced down the steps to the sidewalk.

Kyle grabbed a yellow bag.

So did Akimi.

Nobody wanted to fly all the way to Columbus to learn about Lincoln, even if they could take the private jet, not if Mr. Lemoncello's fun fact could be found faster by bike.

Kyle and Abia scurried away from Angus and Akimi, who were scurrying away from them. Both teams huddled over their backpacks and searched through the pockets and flaps looking for a clue.

They couldn't find one!

Kyle looked down the sidewalk at Akimi and Angus. They were stumped, too.

That's when everybody's IPads started buzzing. A text message scrolled across the screen:

I told you I get tired of the same old, same old.

This was followed by another text:

Here comes your clue.

And another.

Get ready for it.

And several more:

Any second now.

Mr. Lincoln is bummed nobody wants to find his fact.

I reminded him that most folks are about as happy as they make up their minds to be.

Where did I put that clue?

Ah! Here it is!

The tablet screen filled with a jumble of letters:

OH THE PLACE YOU SHOULD GO
In Nine Hidden Words

```
O  F  T  Q  Y  E  P  W  J  O
C  L  D  Q  M  I  O  M  W  L
H  U  L  O  T  X  P  T  G  F
I  C  H  E  D  H  L  N  H  N
L  G  J  U  C  G  A  W  L  B
D  Z  E  K  Y  N  R  V  A  D
H  C  A  X  O  L  O  O  E  I
O  S  Y  S  Z  H  A  M  N  Z
O  L  I  T  T  L  E  T  E  E
D  J  N  E  N  A  L  D  I  L
```

"It's a classic word search," Kyle told Abia. "Start circling!"

"I found 'Lemoncello,'" said Abia. "It starts in the lower right corner and runs in a backward diagonal to the upper left!"

"Excellent."

They both started circling words with their fingertips. The circled letters changed color and flashed when they were correct. Down at the other end of the sidewalk, Akimi and Angus were doing the same thing.

In about three minutes, Kyle and Abia had discovered all nine words in the ten-by-ten box:

CHILDHOOD
HOME
ITALY
LANE
LEMONCELLO
LITTLE
ONE
POPLAR
TWO

"When Mr. Lemoncello was little, was his home in Italy?" asked Abia.

"No," said Kyle. "His 'childhood' 'home' was right here in Alexandriaville. In a neighborhood called 'Little' 'Italy.' There's a street in that part of town named 'Poplar' 'Lane.'"

"So," said Abia, tapping the words "one" and "two" on her screen, "he either lived at Twelve Poplar Lane or Twenty-One Poplar Lane."

"Come on," said Kyle. "Let's grab a bike. Twelve and Twenty-One have to be pretty close to each other, maybe even on the same block."

They hurried to the bikes.

Just in time to see Akimi and Angus already pedaling away.

27

Akimi and Angus were in the lead as the four bikes raced across town.

"I know a shortcut!" Kyle hollered to Abia.

"Of course you do!" Abia shouted back.

He swung down Birch Street to cross the train tracks. Abia followed him.

They made it to Poplar before Akimi and Angus. The street was lined with simple brownstone apartment buildings, five stories tall.

"There's Twenty-One," said Abia. "How do we know if that was Mr. Lemoncello's childhood home?"

"Maybe there's a plaque or something. . . ."

They propped their bikes on their kickstands and hurried up the stoop to the front door to see if they could find some sort of sign labeling it as the childhood home of the most famous son of Alexandriaville, Ohio.

"Hey, look!" someone shouted. "Here's a plaque! 'Boyhood home of master game maker Luigi L. Lemoncello'!"

It was Angus, up the block on the other side of the street at *12* Poplar Lane.

He and Akimi were on the stoop with a sweet-looking old lady in a black housecoat who'd come out to greet them.

"*Buongiorno!* Welcome to my nephew little Luigi's childhood home. Come in, come in. I have almond biscotti upstairs."

"Thank you, ma'am," Kyle heard Angus say, "but we're kind of in a hurry. May not have time for a snack."

"But you are so skinny. . . ."

"They're going in," said Abia.

"Um, ma'am?" shouted Kyle. "We'd like to see the house, too."

"You're gonna have to wait," said the lady. "I can only do one tour at a time. My feet are killing me."

Angus waved a twiddle-fingered "buh-bye" to Kyle. He and Akimi hurried into Mr. Lemoncello's childhood home with their tour guide.

"Come on," Kyle said to Abia. "We'll search the outside of the building while we wait."

They biked down the block.

The brownstone behind the rusting wrought-iron fence looked so cramped, Kyle couldn't imagine Mr. Lemoncello living there with his nine brothers and sisters.

"Hmm," said Abia, "look at this. Someone has scratched a strange and nonsensical message into this fence post."

Kyle bent down and examined the etching:

!KNIHT FLESYM RAEH OT DEEN I

"It could be some kind of code," said Kyle. "Mr. Lemoncello loves secret codes. Always has. Even when he was a little kid. The first game he ever tried to make was called First Letters, where . . ."

Kyle stopped.

"It's like 'Lemoncello' from the word jumble and 'open sesame' on his front door. It's backward. 'I need to hear myself think!' "

"What does it mean?"

"That *we* need to race back to the library!"

"Why?"

Kyle was so glad he'd just done that school report on Mr. Lemoncello.

"His childhood home was so crowded and noisy, the public library was the only place where the twelve-year-old Luigi could 'hear himself think' and work on his game ideas!"

"Excellent research analysis, Kyle Keeley!"

They hopped onto their bikes and, pumping hard, made it back to the library in record time. When they bounded up the front steps and into the lobby, Mr. Lemoncello wasn't there.

But his hologram generated by the Nonfictionator was.

"Do you like the semitransparent me?" asked the Lemoncello illusion. "The real me used the three-D camera hidden inside the beak of a ceramic raven in his office to pose for me. I think I look a lot like me, don't you? The ear, the eye, *and* the arm. I sound like me, too, because that was a book title I just cleverly dropped into my speech."

"Um, this is all great, Mr., uh, Fake Lemoncello," said Kyle. "But we found a clue at your childhood home that sent us back here. . . ."

"As it should've!" replied the hologram. "There is one fascinating fact missing from my database, because, well, I'm embarrassed to say, the real Mr. Lemoncello forgot to tell the equally real Mr. Raymo the inspiration for my very first board game."

"Your family!" said Kyle, surprised at how easy the answer was.

"Can you give me names? Because as a data-driven interactive device, I need details, specifics, and, most important, data!"

"Come on," Kyle said to Abia. "We'll look upstairs. The Lemoncello-abilia Room. There's probably a family scrapbook or Bible with all the names listed inside it."

Kyle and Abia hurried up the grand staircase to the second floor and made their way around the balcony to a spiral staircase they could take to the third floor.

They burst into the Lemoncello-abilia Room, which

was cluttered with a mishmash of knickknacks and souvenirs from Mr. Lemoncello's past.

"Dig in!" said Kyle as he started pawing his way through the piles of unorganized junk. It was more cluttered than his grandmother's attic (which was more cluttered than his grandfather's workbench). Kyle found a stack of antique comic books. A bag full of brightly colored tiddledywinks. A snow globe from the 1964 New York World's Fair.

"Is this the game referred to in Mr. Lemoncello's question?" asked Abia as she pulled out a long, slender box that had been jammed between two big cardboard crates.

"No," said Kyle. "Mr. Lemoncello's game is called Family Frenzy, not Family Frolic. There's no Imagination Factory logo in the corner, either. That's not even a Lemoncello game."

"So what is it doing in the Lemoncello-abilia Room?"

"Good question."

Curious, Kyle studied the box top. There was a photograph of a young woman with a bright smile, heavy black eye makeup, and blond hair that curled in to brush her apple cheeks. The words "Family Frolic" bounced across the box in letters that reminded Kyle of the titles from that 1960s TV show *Gilligan's Island,* which he'd checked out on YouTube after hearing Emily Dickinson sing her poem.

"Have fun frolicking with my groovy family!" was written in a cartoon balloon coming out of the blond lady's smile.

Kyle lifted off the lid and unfolded the game board.

"Wow. It looks almost exactly like Family Frenzy. See, there's the apartment building, the church, and the dog pound. Here's Millionaire's Mansion. Huh. One of the playing pieces is a red boot. Another is a pouncing cat."

"Those are both in Family Frenzy, are they not?" asked Abia.

"Yeah," said Kyle as he riffled through the deck of game cards.

While he did that, Abia examined the inside of the box top.

"You are assessed fifty dollars for sewer repairs," said Kyle, reading the top card. "There's one just like that in Family Frenzy. Somebody stole Mr. Lemoncello's idea!"

"When did Family Frenzy first come out?" asked Abia.

"I don't know, exactly." Kyle looked around the room and saw a dusty heap of antique Lemoncello board games, including a classic edition of Family Frenzy.

He opened the game and read the information printed inside the box lid. "Copyright Luigi L. Lemoncello, 1974."

Abia had a sad look on her face.

"What?" asked Kyle. "What's wrong?"

Abia read what was printed inside the lid of the Family Frolic box: "Family Frolic. Copyright Irma Hirschman, 1969."

"Impossible," said Kyle. "That was five years *before* Mr. Lemoncello invented it."

"Exactly," said Abia. "Perhaps, given his devotion to

the truth, this is the answer Mr. Lemoncello wanted us to find—the one he was too 'embarrassed' to tell Mr. Raymo. The inspiration for his first game may very well have been a game created five years earlier by Irma Hirschman."

"What? You think *he* stole the idea from *her*? That Mr. Lemoncello made his first millions with someone else's game?"

"I think we need to do more research to learn the truth. Or we could race back downstairs and give our first answer: It *seems* the inspiration for Family Frenzy was Family Frolic, a game created by a woman named Irma Hirschman in 1969."

"But that can't be true," said Kyle. "Can it?"

28

While Kyle and Abia sat in the Lemoncello-abilia Room contemplating their next move, Akimi and Angus came flying through the door.

They were both out of breath from running so hard.

"Your clues sent you up here, too?" asked Akimi.

"Yeah," said Kyle as he mindlessly set up the playing pieces and cards for Family Frenzy on what had once been the Lemoncellos' kitchen table. He'd placed the Lemoncello board game next to Irma Hirschman's Family Frolic so he could make a detailed, side-by-side comparison.

"Did y'all find the answer?" asked Angus.

"Maybe," said Abia, handing the Family Frolic box lid to Akimi and Angus.

"We don't like what we found," added Kyle.

Akimi flipped the Family Frolic lid back and forth a few times.

"Why are you guys even bothering with this game?" she asked. "It's not a Lemoncello. It's from some bubble-haired blond lady named Irma Hirschman. She looks like she's going to a 1960s costume party as Doris Day."

"I beg your pardon?" said Abia.

"We had a sixties theme at school a couple years ago. I wore tie-dye. Haley Daley went as Doris Day."

Akimi set down the box top and stared at Kyle, who had his head in his hands while he studied the two game boards.

"Oh-kay," she said. "You're certainly acting weird today. You needed to stop and play some 'groovy' 1960s game in the middle of our Fabulous Fact-Finding Frenzy because . . . ?"

"I believe Kyle Keeley needs some time to think," said Abia.

"Oh, really?" scoffed Angus. "Well, *we* need a list of names for the rest of Luigi's brothers and sisters. His aunt gave us Massimo, Francesca, and Fabio at the apartment."

"We need six more," said Akimi. "Plus, his father's and mother's names."

"His aunt told us his mom's name was Angelica," added Angus. "But, like all good researchers, we want to verify her statement with a second source."

"There might be a family Bible over there in that stack of books," said Kyle, gesturing limply, his eyes still glued to the two game boards.

"Good idea," said Angus. "A lot of families inscribe

the names of their children and ancestors in the front of a Bible on a family tree."

Akimi and Angus rushed to the stack of books.

And froze.

"Wait a dadgum second," said Angus. "If you two know where and how to find the answer, plus you had a ten-minute jump on us, why didn't you just go ahead, jot down what was in the Lemoncello family tree, and win this thing?"

"They're trying to fake us out!" said Akimi. "Very clever, Kyle. Come on—for years you've told me Mr. Lemoncello based his first game on his big, crazy Italian family. If that's the right answer, why didn't you guys do the Bible family tree thing yourselves?"

Kyle didn't answer. He robotically rolled some dice and moved the boot token around the Family Frolic board.

"He even got the boot from her," he mumbled. "There has to be some mistake. Mr. Lemoncello would never do something like that. . . ."

"Hello?" said Akimi. "Earth to Kyle. What are you mumbling about?"

Abia sighed. "We are afraid," she said, "that 'Mr. Lemoncello's family'—with a list of the names of his parents, brothers, and sisters—may not be the correct answer to the question 'Who or what was the inspiration for his very first board game?'"

She picked up the lid for Family Frolic that Akimi had dropped.

"It appears as if Mr. Lemoncello may have received the inspiration for his game from a very similar game that was invented five years earlier by a woman named Irma Hirschman, who apparently looked like this Doris Day you spoke of."

"He stole the idea?" said Angus.

"So it would seem," said Abia.

"No," said Kyle. "It's not right."

"Well, duh," said Angus. "That's why they call stealing stuff a crime!"

"But Mr. Lemoncello wouldn't do that. He has so many ideas of his own. He doesn't need to steal them from somebody else. . . ."

"Akimi?" said Angus. "What the heck are we waiting for?"

"Hang on," said Kyle, snapping out of his funk. "This could ruin Mr. Lemoncello."

"So?" said Angus. "Facts are facts. It's like that deal with Thomas Edison and the lightbulb."

"You're jumping to conclusions," said Kyle.

Akimi couldn't help but smile. "Something you know how to do better than anybody, Kyle."

"True. But . . ."

"But what?" said Angus.

"Well, what if Mr. Lemoncello isn't the one who put this board game in this room? What if somebody did it just to make him look bad? We need to dig deeper."

"No. We don't," said Angus. "We need to win! Come on, Akimi."

She didn't budge. "Kyle is right. Stealing ideas? Plagiarism? Those are major accusations, Angus. We could destroy Mr. Lemoncello, his game company, this library—everything."

"But," said Angus, "what if it *is* true?"

"What if it's not?" demanded Kyle. "We owe it to Mr. Lemoncello to examine all the facts, not just a box lid. The way I see it, he's innocent until totally proven guilty. We should ask for a delay so we can do more research."

"If both teams ask for a postponement," said Akimi, "I bet they'll give it to us."

"And then what?" said Angus.

"The four of us investigate further," said Abia.

"And when the four of us find the truth," asked Angus, "who gets to race back here, give the correct answer, and win the game?"

Kyle looked at Abia.

She nodded.

He turned back to face Angus and Akimi.

"You guys," he said.

29

"Right here's your answer," said Angus.

The four remaining data dashers had gone into the Young Adult Room on the third floor to use one of the computers.

"Justice for Irma dot org. The whole ugly story is laid out for everybody to see."

Kyle looked at the screen. There was a grainy black-and-white photo of a sweet little old lady wearing granny glasses and an apron over a checked gingham dress. Her gray hair was pinned up in a bun shaped like a cheese Danish.

"Guess she got old," said Akimi.

"She's a granny," added Angus.

"Yeah," said Kyle. "She sort of looks like one of those Mrs. Maplebutter syrup bottles."

She also looked extremely sad in the photograph as she held up her 1969 Family Frolic game board with one hand while pointing to the Family Frenzy board spread out on a table in front of her.

"This is horrible," said Akimi, reading the text next to the photograph:

> In 1969, Irma Hirschman, now a kindly grandmother residing in Smithville, Missouri, was working as a stenographer when she created a board game she called Family Frolic.
>
> "It was based on my happy memories of my big family. I wanted to share that joy and cheerfulness with children all around the world."
>
> Her simple game, with its race from the Local Neighborhood to My First Job to Baby Makes Three to Millionaire's Mansion, was never a huge hit, but several copies, all manufactured by a local printer in Smithville, were sold by a traveling salesman to homes in the American Midwest.
>
> "I guess that peddler sold a game or two up in Ohio," Mrs. Hirschman remarked over tea in a recent interview. This interviewer paid for the tea, as Mrs. Hirschman is currently living in a homeless shelter. "That's where little Luigi first got his sticky fingers on my game."
>
> Five years later, Mr. Lemoncello, the

zany billionaire game maker, took Family Frolic and turned it into Family Frenzy.

"He tells everybody that the game was based on *his* big Italian family," said Mrs. Hirschman, sniffling away her tears, the tears she has been shedding for over four decades. "He says some local librarian helped him put together the prototype, lending him charms from her bracelet and trinkets she had tucked away in her desk drawer to use as playing pieces. That she even gave him a Barbie doll boot! But the truth is the truth. He stole my game. He stole my memories. He even stole my boot! When I called his big, fancy company—the Imagination Factory in New York City—to complain, those city slickers hung up on me!"

Mr. Lemoncello's entire multibillion-dollar fortune was built on the success of his debut board game, Family Frenzy.

He has never shared a penny of his profits with Mrs. Hirschman, now seventy-five years old, who currently gets by on Social Security, disability insurance, food stamps, and "the kindness of my neighbors here in Smithville and its lovely homeless shelter."

"Man," said Angus. "Who does Mr. Lemoncello think he is? That is one hundred percent disgusting!"

"Only if it's true," said Kyle angrily.

"Hey, we have two sources. The box lid and this website."

"Neither of which should be considered completely reliable," said Abia.

Angus blew her a raspberry. "What? Somebody dummied up this board game and planted it here at the library while somebody else posted a bogus website?"

"It's a possibility!" insisted Kyle.

"Wait a second," said Angus. "There's a link to Mr. Lemoncello's Wikipedia page." Angus clicked the mouse. "Oh, snap. Mr. L got kicked out of high school for cheating at chess? He was one seriously bad dude when he was a kid. Cheating, stealing . . ."

"Anyone can edit a Wikipedia entry," said Akimi.

Angus leaned back in his beanbag chair. "Look, I know you guys are locals. . . ."

"I'm not," said Abia.

"Okay. Fine. Y'all just love Mr. Lemoncello. Heck, I do, too. I mean, I did. But face it, the truth is the truth."

"I don't know," said Akimi. "This whole thing smells like the dumpster behind a Long John Silver's to me."

"Fishy?" said Abia.

"Exactly."

Kyle felt sick to his stomach (and not because of Akimi's stinky fish thing).

"Look, Angus," he said, "if this truth is somehow actually the truth, it'll still be true tomorrow, right?"

"Unless somebody edits the Wikipedia page again," cracked Akimi.

"I still believe in Mr. Lemoncello, and I am not ready to ruin his reputation," said Kyle. "Not without more facts."

"Me neither," said Akimi.

"I concur," added Abia. "We should dig deeper."

"Fine," said Angus. "Let's go ask the holographic Lemoncello for a delay of game. But when we find out the truth . . ."

"You and Akimi win," said Kyle. "A deal's a deal. You two can be the ones who go on tour with all the new Lemoncello Library exhibits."

"I don't know," sighed Akimi. "If this Irma Hirschman stuff is true, there may not be a Lemoncello Library anymore."

On their way down to the lobby to ask for some extra time, Kyle realized that if all the Irma Hirschman stuff was really true and it forced Mr. Lemoncello out of town, he and Akimi would miss Mr. Lemoncello more than Abia and Angus would.

"We've been with him since he opened this library," said Kyle.

"Yep," said Akimi. "And we might be here when he closes it, too. Especially if people like the Chiltingtons find out he stole his first game idea."

"They wouldn't force Mr. Lemoncello to close the library for theft of intellectual property," said Angus. "They'd just take his name off the door and ask him to never come back."

"They would probably remove his statue as well," said Abia.

"True," said Angus. "And for sure they'd close up that Lemoncello-abilia Room."

"And take away his private suite."

"Then they'd want to get rid of all those board games in the boardroom and—"

"Okay, okay, you guys," said Akimi. "We get the picture."

Kyle knew the truth: Without Mr. Lemoncello, the library would still be a library. It just wouldn't be Mr. Lemoncello's library.

The glittering Lemoncello hologram was still standing where they'd left him. But his eyes were closed. And he was snoring.

"Um, excuse me?" Kyle said to the snoozing hologram.

The fake Mr. Lemoncello's eyes popped open. "Oh, hello. You were gone so long I must've entered my sleep mode. Do you have an answer? Why aren't you standing on the lemon square? Would you like a recipe for lemon squares?" The hologram sputtered. "Bob Lemon was an all-star Major League Baseball pitcher who had his heyday in the 1940s and fifties."

The Nonfictionator random access memory chips were acting a little too randomly.

"Whoa, hang on," said Angus.

"We need to discuss something with you," said Akimi, looking around and seeing regular library patrons starting to stream into the building. "In private."

"We can use Meeting Room A," suggested Kyle.

"Wonderrific!" said the hologram.

Then it disappeared with a squiggle-blip.

"Guess the Nonfictionator is sending him to Meeting Room A," said Kyle. "Let's go."

Kyle, Akimi, Angus, and Abia went into the rotunda and over to the door to Meeting Room A.

It was locked.

"This meeting room is reserved for the holographic Mr. Lemoncello and his guests," said the voice in the ceiling. "Please enter the door code to gain access."

There was an alphanumeric pad, like on a telephone, above the door handle.

"Great," said Akimi. "Anybody know the pass code?"

"Yep," said Kyle. "The same one he uses for every lock, remember?"

He quickly tapped 7-3-2-3, because those numbers shared key space with the letters R-E-A-D.

The door opened. The group stepped in.

The Lemoncello hologram wasn't in the meeting room, but Mr. Lemoncello was.

Well, his face, anyway. It was filling one of the room's walls, which doubled as a video screen. And it was a worried face—without the usual twinkle in the eyes.

"Um, hello, sir," said Kyle. "All of us in the Fabulous Fact-Finding Frenzy would like to request a delay of game."

"Why?" asked Mr. Lemoncello. "Is it raining?"

"No," said Abia. "Both teams need additional research time."

"Because," said Kyle, "we don't want to jump to conclusions."

Mr. Lemoncello nodded. "Probably a wise move. Conclusion-jumping often leads to bad answers and twisted ankles."

"We want to make sure we know the truth, the whole truth, and nothing but the truth," added Angus.

"So do I," said Mr. Lemoncello, "even if it takes a year down yonder. Therefore, your request is hereby granted."

"We might also need your jet," said Akimi. "In case we have to, you know, fly someplace."

Mr. Lemoncello nodded knowingly. "One often does when on a quest for truth. Use whatever tools it takes. Now, if you will excuse me, I have to talk to a detective who reminds me a bit of Timmy Failure when we need Encyclopedia Brown. I suspect mistakes will be made."

"A detective?" said Angus. "What's going on?"

"Oh, nothing much. It seems I've been burgled. Someone cracked open my super-secure floor safe."

"Did they take anything?" asked Kyle.

"Yes, Kyle. That's why we call it a burglary. If they didn't burgle anything, we'd simply call it an uninvited guest."

"What did they pilfer?" asked Abia.

"My future. They stole the complete set of plans to my Fantabulous Floating Emoji game. My big hit for the holidays has gone missing!"

31

"Finding the truth, no matter what truth you are seeking, is more important than finding the thief who stole my blueprints," said Mr. Lemoncello when Kyle suggested they should call off the whole Fabulous Fact-Finding Frenzy.

So, early the next morning, the four remaining contestants met at the library to discuss their research strategy.

"We need to get to the bottom of this," said Kyle. "Fast."

"Where do we start?" asked Angus.

"The heart of his game-making empire," suggested Abia. "New York City. Home of Mr. Lemoncello's Imagination Factory!"

"Good idea," said Akimi. "If this Irma Hirschman called them, like she claims she did on her website, somebody at his I.F. headquarters may have already found the answer we're searching for."

151

With the permission of Ms. Waintraub, the holographic research librarian, they brought the Family Frolic board game they'd found in the Lemoncello-abilia Room with them.

Mad Dog drove them back to the airport.

"Do you have your permission slips?" asked the flight attendant on Mr. Lemoncello's private jet.

They all handed over their signed scrolls.

"Our parents are behind us one hundred percent," said Kyle.

"Then buckle up!"

Nobody was interested in all the free food on the flight from Ohio to New York. They were too busy working their armrest computers, digging for information, searching for the truth.

"This is good," said Akimi, scrolling through a website. "It says here you can always tell when someone's lying because they touch or cover their mouths. They also shuffle their feet, point a lot, and stare at you without blinking."

Kyle nodded. "Good to know when we start talking to people in New York. Some of Mr. Lemoncello's employees may not want to tell us the truth. It could cost them their jobs."

"Fascinating," said Abia, clacking keys on her computer.

"What'd you find?" asked Kyle.

"It's more what I did *not* find. Google allows you to

call up patents quite easily. For instance, I found Charles B. Darrow's patent filing from 1935 for his 'board game apparatus' Monopoly. I also located Luigi L. Lemoncello's 1974 patent for Family Frenzy, complete with a full description of the board, game cards, playing pieces—everything."

"And Family Frolic?" asked Kyle.

"Nothing."

"Maybe Irma Hirschman called the game something else when she filed her patent," suggested Angus.

"I investigated that possibility as well. Still nothing. There are no patents registered to anyone named Irma Hirschman."

"So the game you guys found in the Lemoncello-abilia Room could be a phony?" said Akimi.

"It is a possibility," said Abia.

"Hot dog!" said Kyle.

Akimi cocked an eyebrow. "Since when do you say 'hot dog' when you're pumped instead of 'booyah'?"

Kyle grinned. "I only said 'hot dog' because all of a sudden I'm starving. I'm hoping they still have some of those Chicago-style wieners on board."

When the banana jet landed at a corporate airfield just outside of New York City, a limousine, molded and painted to look like a harmonica on wheels (because a tiny tin harmonica was another one of the tokens you could pick when playing Family Frenzy), pulled right up to the jet's steps.

"Welcome," said the driver. "You kids have any luggage?"

"Just this," said Kyle, gesturing with the Family Frolic game box.

The driver took off his sunglasses and somberly studied the box top.

"Family Frolic. Is that the game the lady from Missouri invented before the boss invented his version of the same game?"

"Well," said Akimi, "that's what somebody wants us to believe."

"Yeah," said the driver, pointing over his shoulder with his thumb. "Irma Hirschman. She's been on talk radio all morning, sobbing and sniffling and telling anybody who will listen that Mr. Lemoncello stole her idea."

Kyle and the others hurried into the limo.

"Here she is again," said the driver, dialing up the volume on his radio. "They play this sound bite like every ten minutes."

"After all these years, I've finally found the courage to speak up," said a sweet-sounding voice. "The gals in my quilting bee at the retirement home convinced me that it's never too late to tell the truth. Mr. Lemoncello stole my idea. He should've been punished decades ago. But better late than never."

"Retirement home?" said Akimi. "I thought she lived in a homeless shelter."

"You guys?" said Kyle. "This is way too big of a

coincidence. Yesterday we find Irma Hirschman's board game. Today she's all over the radio crying about it?"

"Too bad it's radio," said Akimi. "If it were TV, we could see her covering her mouth, shuffling her feet, *and* staring without blinking!"

Kyle really hoped Akimi was right.

He hoped Irma Hirschman was totally lying.

32

Everything about Mr. Lemoncello's Imagination Factory world headquarters in New York City was wild and wacky.

The front wall of the building at Sixth Avenue and Twenty-Third Street, in the heart of downtown Manhattan, was filled with grand columns, incredible arches, and wildly imaginative gargoyles—including several that were chiseled to look like Mr. Lemoncello wearing a hooded monk's robe, his nose stuck in a stone book.

There was a balloon store, a bookstore, and a bakery on the ground floor of the block-long office building. The arched golden doorway into the Imagination Factory's lobby was guarded by a pair of mechanical bears in circus band uniforms blowing bubbles out of their trombones.

Once Kyle, Akimi, Angus, and Abia stepped into the lobby, they smelled cotton candy, popcorn, and caramel apples—even though they were nowhere near a county fair.

"They're using Mr. Lemoncello's smell-a-vision technology," said Akimi. She pointed to a placard on an easel where the smells of the week were outlined. Today's theme was "The Circus Is in Town." Tomorrow would be "Chocolate-Dipped Fruit Day." The day after that was "A Scentsational Tribute to American Bubble Gum."

Robots, similar to the ones working at Mr. Lemoncello's library, whizzed across the lobby's shiny floor, silently whisking baskets of mail and trays filled with important packages to wherever they were supposed to go.

A man named Vader Nix, whose parents had been huge Star Wars fans, was the head of marketing and advertising at the Imagination Factory. Kyle had called Mr. Nix when the banana jet began its descent into the New York area. Mr. Nix knew Kyle and Akimi from their star turns in Mr. Lemoncello's holiday commercials (their prize for winning the escape game back when the library first opened). He stepped out of a glass elevator (designed to look like a rocket ship) to greet them.

"Welcome to Lemoncello world headquarters," said Mr. Nix. "I wish you kids could've come on a happier day."

He gestured over his shoulder to a giant brass meter mounted on a wall beneath a mural depicting all the crazy characters and screwy playing pieces from the Lemoncello universe of games. The meter looked like the floor indicator on an old-fashioned elevator, but instead of pointing to a half circle of numbers, the ornately scrolled hand dipped

157

from a toothy happy face past a closed-mouth-smile happy face to a straight-line-mouth semihappy face.

If it nudged much farther to the left, Mr. Lemoncello's Universal Happiness Meter might plunge all the way to frowny face and then angry/snarly face.

"It appears everyone in the world heard Irma Hirschman on the radio this morning," said Abia.

"Did Mr. L come with you kids?" asked Mr. Nix.

Kyle shook his head. "He's still in Ohio. Talking to the police."

"About this Irma Hirschman brouhaha?"

"No. Someone stole the blueprints for his Fantabulous Floating Emoji game."

"And I didn't think it could get any worse." Mr. Nix showed the kids the cover of a special edition of *Game Maker* magazine. "Hot off the presses. It just came out this morning."

The magazine had Mr. Lemoncello illustrated like the Mr. Moneybags character from Monopoly being hauled off by a billy-club-wielding cop—just like on the classic "Go Directly to Jail" Chance card. The headline was horrifying:

MR. LEMONCELLO'S IMAGINATION FACTORY BUILT ON LIES, DECEIT, AND THEFT OF INTELLECTUAL PROPERTY

"Have you heard from this Irma Hirschman before?" asked Kyle.

"Nope. Never."

"She says she called you guys," said Akimi, watching to see if Mr. Nix tried to touch or cover his mouth. He didn't.

"Nobody here has ever heard of her."

"She's never made these claims before?" asked Abia. "She's never sued Mr. Lemoncello?"

"Nope," said Mr. Nix. "But now the accusation is spreading like warm butter on hot waffles."

"That's why we're here," said Kyle. "To prove that Irma Hirschman is a liar."

"Has anybody seen her shuffling her feet a lot lately?" asked Akimi.

"Huh?" said Mr. Nix.

"Never mind," said Akimi. "Her feet aren't our top priority."

"However," said Abia, "her allegations are."

"True," said Mr. Nix, checking his phone, which was buzzing in his palm. "Great. Another tweet. This one takes a swipe at you, too, Kyle."

"What?"

Mr. Nix showed the four of them the tweet, from @SirCharlesThe1st:

@MrLemoncello IS a liar and cheat. He helped super loser @KyleKeeley cheat his way to victory in the escape game!

"Chiltington," said Akimi through clenched teeth.

"Whoa," said Angus. "He's totally trashing you, dude."

"Yeah, well, who cares?" blustered Kyle. "It's not true."

"That may not matter," said Abia. "If Charles Chiltington says it loud enough and often enough, it will seem true."

"I figure that's what Irma Hirschman is trying to do, too," said Mr. Nix. "She probably wants us to offer her a cash settlement. That's why she's screaming so loudly. Unfortunately, it's working. Hashtag JusticeForIrma is trending like crazy. Toy stores have been calling the sales department all morning to cancel orders."

Kyle heard a ding behind Mr. Nix.

The Universal Happiness Meter had just dipped into the frowny-face zone.

33

"Very sorry you kids had to visit on such a terrible, horrible, no good, very bad day," said Mr. Nix.

It made Kyle smile.

Because suddenly Vader Nix sounded like Mr. Lemoncello.

"Who do you think we should talk to?" he asked.

"Max Khatchadourian, our corporate lawyer," replied Mr. Nix. "He's been with Mr. Lemoncello since day one. If anyone's ever heard of this Irma Hirschman or her allegations, it'd be Max." He glanced at his watch. "Max should just be getting to his desk."

"Really?" said Akimi. "It's like eleven o'clock."

"Mr. L lets Max set his own hours."

"He likes to sleep in?" asked Angus.

"Exactly."

"I can relate."

"If we hurry," said Mr. Nix, "we can catch Max before he starts returning all the calls that have been coming in all morning. *Everybody* wants to talk to Mr. Lemoncello's lawyer!"

Mr. Nix led the kids onto an elevator.

As it rocketed from the lobby to the fifth floor, Kyle barely noticed the chirping flock of holographic bluebirds swirling around the car's glass exterior. Or the caped superhero propelling the express elevator that passed them on the left. He was too focused on Mr. Lemoncello. He had to protect his hero!

The doors slid open, and Mr. Nix led the way down a cramped corridor cluttered with musty boxes.

They came to a frosted glass door filled with hand-painted writing: "Max Khatchadourian, Chief Corporate Counsel (Except for Nitpicky Legal Matters Regarding Dotted i's and Crossed t's That He's Far Too Old to Be Bothered With)." Kyle could hear a phone ringing on the other side of the door. Somebody picked it up. And slammed it back down.

Mr. Nix rapped his knuckles on the glass.

"Come in, come in," cried a chipper, creaky voice.

Mr. Nix pushed open the door. He had to shove it hard because there was a mountain of cardboard boxes stacked behind it on the floor. In fact, Kyle couldn't even see Mr. Lemoncello's top lawyer until they found a clear alleyway between all the boxes and stacks of papers.

"Hello, Max," said Mr. Nix. "These are some members of Luigi's board of trustees out in Ohio."

Max Khatchadourian looked like a withered elf in a robin's-egg-blue business suit. His shirt collar was two sizes too big for his skinny neck, and his striped tie was three times wider than the ones most people wore. He was unplugging the wire on the back of his telephone. Probably so it would stop ringing.

"Ah, Ohio," said Mr. Khatchadourian, his ancient eyes brightening. "The Buckeye State, where in 1869, W. F. Semple patented chewing gum and in 1974 a brilliant young lad with a quick wit and a wild sense of humor named Luigi Libretto Lemoncello patented a board game titled Family Frenzy. Given its historical significance to this company and the fun-loving world, that first patent, and all the supporting materials related to it, is presently enshrined in the archives of Mr. Lemoncello's Library. I rest my case."

Mr. Khatchadourian folded his hands over his lap, leaned back in his padded office chair, and smiled contentedly.

"Um, that's sort of why we are here," said Kyle.

"I see," said Mr. Khatchadourian. "Do you have a board game you want me to patent for you, too? If so, I must say I am quite impressed. You are even younger than Luigi was when he first traipsed into my office with a battered shoebox filled with trinkets, taped-together

163

cardboard sheets, dice, and dreams. I remember he had one of Barbie's go-go boots in that box. That turned into the boot token, of course. Then there were the tiny buildings he carved out of balsa wood. . . ."

"We're here to talk about the woman who claims Mr. Lemoncello stole his idea from her," said Angus.

"Have you ever seen this, sir?" asked Abia, handing the lawyer the Family Frolic board game.

"No, I have not. But who, may I ask, is this fetching young woman with the bobbed blond hair on the box top?"

"That's Irma Hirschman," said Angus. "She's the one claiming she invented Family Frolic back in 1969—five years before Mr. Lemoncello created Family Frenzy."

"In 1969, eh? That would explain the hairdo."

"But," said Abia, "there is no record of Ms. Hirschman ever filing for a patent."

Mr. Khatchadourian examined the Family Frolic box top.

"We suspect she is fabricating her charges against Mr. Lemoncello," Abia continued. "We also suspect that someone fabricated this board game."

"And I suspect that you are correct," said the lawyer. "I have been with Mr. Lemoncello for a very long time. No one named Irma Hirschman has ever claimed that we stole her idea or dragged us into a court of law. . . ."

"True," said Mr. Nix. "But right now she's giving us a good thrashing in the court of public opinion."

"As might be expected," said Mr. Khatchadourian.

"Public opinion can often be swayed by emotion with little regard for facts. If the story is fascinating enough, facts may not matter to those hearing it. However, if Ms. Hirschman really had a case, she would've sued Luigi years ago. Besides, her hair is far too blond."

"Excuse me?" said Mr. Nix.

Mr. Khatchadourian opened a desk drawer and pulled out a framed, if faded, photograph.

"This is me in 1970. My college formal. My date for the evening, a lovely young gal named Heather Newton, had the most gorgeous golden ringlets. Unfortunately that color has faded from this photograph, if not my memory."

Everybody in the room was staring and nodding.

Mr. Khatchadourian sounded kind of kooky.

"Um, that's very interesting, Max," said Mr. Nix. "But I'm not really clear how it's relevant."

Mr. Khatchadourian smiled. "If my cherished photograph, printed in 1970, has lost so much of its color, why is Ms. Hirschman's golden hair so bright and vibrant on this box top? Why, the colors are so rich and crisp, it looks like it was printed last week. Perhaps because it was."

"I knew it!" said Kyle. "That game board is a fake. Somebody made it to ruin Mr. Lemoncello's good name."

Mr. Khatchadourian smiled, leaned back in his chair, and folded his hands in his lap again.

"I rest my case."

34

"Our next step should be tracking down this Irma Hirschman!" said Kyle. "Confronting her with the facts. Telling her she's a phony and a fraud."

Akimi rolled her eyes. "Riiiight. That always works."

Mr. Nix had given the research team from Ohio a conference room they could use on the fifth floor of the Imagination Factory. The table in the center was amazing—a glass-topped gold fish tank.

"Let us analyze the facts we have thus far," said Abia. "We know she never filed for a patent. Mr. Lemoncello, on the other hand, did. We suspect the board game found in the Lemoncello-abilia Room is a recently manufactured fraud."

"We also know this Irma Hirschman character lives in Smithville, Missouri," added Akimi. "Either in a homeless shelter or a retirement home with a quilting bee, whatever that is."

"Trust me," joked Angus, "you do not want to get stung by a quilting bee. *Looooong* stinger."

"Cute, Angus. Cute. But get this—according to our friend Google, the nearest homeless shelters to Smithville are actually in Kansas City."

Angus tapped his lPad tablet computer.

"Nearest airport is in Kansas City, too. We should call the pilot of the banana jet. Have him start working up a flight plan."

"Wait a second," said Kyle. "I'm pretty sure Kansas City is the home of the Krinkle Brothers game company. Katherine Kelly told me."

"This is research," said Akimi, tapping her lPad. "We can't be pretty sure; we need to know."

"Fine. But all I'm saying is if this Irma Hirschman lives a few miles away from the Krinkle brothers' factory, Mr. Lemoncello's number one rivals might be the ones who put her up to all this nonsense."

"Boom," said Akimi, flipping her lPad around so Kyle could see it. "Krinkle Brothers Games and Amusements. 13300 Arlington Road. Grandview, Missouri. That's just south of Kansas City proper."

"This is interesting," mumbled Abia, who was tapping on the keyboard attached to the computer in the conference room.

"What've you got?" asked Akimi as everybody crowded around the screen.

"This Wikipedia entry for Mr. Lemoncello with the story of his childhood cheating at chess as well as a link to the Justice for Irma page are new additions."

"How new?" asked Angus.

"Last week."

"Can we tell who made the edits?" asked Kyle.

"Not really. There is, of course, a tab at the top of the page labeled "history." However, people who are not logged into Wikipedia and wish to remain anonymous often edit articles. Even if the editor is logged in, they may be using a pseudonym. One thing I can tell: These fresh edits were made from a computer inside the Lemoncello Library."

"So," said Kyle, "either Mr. Lemoncello felt extremely guilty last week and made the edits himself . . ."

"A very weird way to confess," added Akimi.

"Or," Kyle continued, "somebody made the changes to the page on a library computer just to make it look like Mr. Lemoncello had finally confessed."

"We need to go to Kansas City," said Angus.

Kyle nodded. "Call the pilot. I'll ask Mr. Nix to find us a ride back to the airport."

One hour later, the four teammates were flying west to Missouri.

Somewhere over Indiana, the computer screens in all the armrests started chirping with an incoming video call.

It was Miguel Fernandez.

"Yo, Kyle. Where are you guys?"

"On our way to Kansas City, Missouri."

"Why?"

"We think that's where we'll find this Irma Hirschman, the one who's making the big stink about Mr. Lemoncello supposedly stealing her game."

Miguel lowered his voice.

"She isn't the only one making a big stink. The mayor's here."

"At the library?"

"Yep. There's a whole bunch of reporters and TV cameras, too. Couple cops. And . . ."

Miguel looked terrified, like he'd just seen a zombie slurping somebody's brain out of an ear.

"Mrs. Chiltington is here, too!"

35

Mrs. Chiltington, Charles's mother, did not like Mr. Lemoncello.

In fact, it would be safe to say she hated, loathed, detested, abhorred, and despised him, which were all the words her son, Charles, would've used to describe how she felt about Kyle's hero.

"Just about all the other players from the Fabulous Fact-Finding Frenzy are here with me," Miguel whispered, panning his lPad around the room. Kyle saw the other contestants ringed around the rotunda looking quite glum: Diane, Pranav, Elliott, Andrew, Sierra, and Jamal.

The only one missing was Katherine Kelly.

"Can you guys hear what Mrs. Chiltington is saying?" asked Andrew, sticking his face in front of the lPad's camera lens.

"Um, not when you're talking and blocking the shot," answered Akimi.

"Oh, right. I'll be quiet. Because here she goes again."

The video image swished to the left to find Mrs. Chiltington, a clump of properly dressed ladies, one properly dressed man in a bow tie, and Mayor O'Brady, who had very puffy hair. The mayor was flanked by a dozen police officers. The Rotunda Reading Room was crammed with curious onlookers and TV camera crews.

On Mr. Lemoncello's corporate jet, everybody (except the pilots, who were sort of busy) gathered around the big TV screen spanning the bulkhead wall, which was displaying the computer feed.

"Those of us in the League of Concerned Library Lovers," warbled Mrs. Chiltington in her operatic voice, "are, frankly, quite concerned. We have heard these accusations made by Irma Hirschman from her cozy retirement home in Missouri."

"Now she lives someplace cozy?" cracked Akimi. "This lady gets around."

Mrs. Chiltington crinkled her nose. "Mr. Lemoncello is a cheap pirate, plagiarizing and pilfering other people's patented, proprietary property."

Her lips exploded with salvos of saliva every time she popped one of those "P" words.

"He's also egregiously malevolent!" shouted Charles, who was sort of stuck behind the blockade of properly dressed ladies.

"To have such a cheat and charlatan affiliated with a library," said Mrs. Chiltington, "let alone running it, is, as my son would say, egregiously improper, intolerable, and offensive."

"It's patently preposterous!" shouted Charles. He spat on people when he popped his "P"s, too.

"Hear, hear," chanted all the properly dressed ladies and the one gentleman in the bow tie.

"We, friends and neighbors, are the laughingstock of the entire state of Ohio, nay, the world!" Mrs. Chiltington said to the crowd. "Oh, how those wags over in Bowling Green are laughing at us now."

"We can't have that," said Mayor O'Brady. "We can't have the whole world laughing at us like that. Not those people in Bowling Green. Not on my watch!"

"Wait a second!" shouted Miguel from the back of the room, because he was brave that way. "Does anybody even know if what this Irma Hirschman is saying is true?"

"Or doesn't the truth matter to you people anymore?" demanded Jamal.

"Yeah!" added Diane Capriola.

"Oh, you poor, poor misguided children," said Mrs. Chiltington, batting her eyelashes and smiling at the seven library trustees in the room as if they were orphans abandoned in baskets on the church steps during a Christmas Eve blizzard. "Mr. Lemoncello has you under his sugar-coated spell. This *is* the truth."

172

Charles Chiltington pushed his way through the wall of scowling women and the pouting man in the bow tie.

He thrust up his cell phone.

"Take a look, people. Irma Hirschman did indeed invent a game called Family Frolic five years before Mr. Lemoncello *theoretically* invented Family Frenzy. I have seen the proof. Two very agreeable elderly gentlemen—brothers, I think—showed it to me one day after they finished using a computer in the Rotunda Reading Room!"

The crowd gasped.

"I photographed the evidence!" cried Charles. "Mr. Lemoncello kept a copy of Ms. Hirschman's board game hidden in his ludicrous Lemoncello-abilia Room—tucked between two big cardboard cartons. Why? Who knows? The man is barmy and batty. Maybe he wanted a souvenir to remind himself how deviously cunning and clever he was in his youth. Maybe he forgot it was up there. Doesn't matter! I took a picture of the game box. A selfie with it, too!"

He wiggle-waggled his camera phone in the air.

"Let's go upstairs and see it!" shouted someone in the crowd.

A mob of people rushed for the steps.

"You can't!" cried Charles. "It's been checked out."

"Huh?" mumbled the mob.

"One of Mr. Lemoncello's favorites, a member of his so-called board of trustees, Kyle Keeley, the loser and cheater Mr. Lemoncello helped beat me in the escape

173

game, conveniently removed the board game so he could 'do research' with it. The robo-research lady told me!"

"That's true," said the holographic research librarian, Ms. Waintraub, who materialized behind the reference desk. "However, it is also true that archival information can, with proper approval, be removed from the Lemoncello-abilia Room for research purposes."

"Or for tossing into the trash!" shouted Charles.

"No," said Ms. Waintraub matter-of-factly. "Tossing into the trash is not an approved use of research materials."

"Enough," said the mayor, raising both of his arms. "We need to get to the bottom of this Irma Hirschman matter. The Lemoncello Library is hereby forthwith closed."

"What?" gasped Sierra Russell. "You can't do that!"

"Oh, yes I can. I am the mayor. I can do all sorts of things. And I will not have anyone in Bowling Green laughing at me. Not again! No, sir!"

The camera whipped around and landed on Miguel's face.

"Yo, did you guys catch all that?"

"Yeah," said Kyle.

"Everybody out of the library!" he heard Mrs. Chiltington bellow in the background. "Now!"

"Hang in there, Miguel," said Kyle. "We're coming home just as soon as we confront Irma Hirschman."

"Hurry!"

36

Once the banana jet landed in Kansas City, it was extremely easy for Kyle and the research team to track down Irma Hirschman.

She had scheduled a press conference.

At the Kansas City Airport Marriott hotel!

Pranav called with the news.

"And get this," he added, "her appearance is being sponsored by the Krinkle brothers."

"What?" said Kyle.

"It's all over Twitter. Those two old farts who do the Whoop Dee Doodle games are the ones who arranged for Ms. Hirschman to meet the press!"

"Two old farts?" said Akimi. "Hello? Charles Chiltington just told the world that 'two very agreeable elderly gentlemen' showed him the Family Frolic board game up in the Lemoncello-abilia Room. 'Elderly gentlemen' is just a smarmier way of saying 'old farts.' "

"I knew they were behind all this!" said Kyle. "They probably showed Chiltington the phony game board right after they got done using a library computer to put that phony junk on Mr. Lemoncello's Wikipedia page!"

"Knowing it is not enough," said Abia. "We must prove it. A confession from Irma Hirschman might be our swiftest route to the truth."

"Yeah, yeah, yeah," said Akimi. "She's right. Let's go."

They had decided that Kyle, Akimi, and Angus would go to the airport hotel to hear what Irma Hirschman had to say, maybe ask her a few questions. Abia would stay on the jet and use its computers to do more Internet research.

"We'll need to zip back to Ohio just as soon as we hear what lies are being spread today," Angus told the pilot.

"Already working up the flight plan," the pilot said with a nod.

"Thanks," said Kyle. "Come on, you guys. We only have like fifteen minutes to find the hotel ballroom where she's speaking!"

The hotel was less than a mile away from the airport terminal. Fortunately the Marriott had a shuttle bus.

The three Lemoncello trustees raced through the lobby and followed the crowd squeezing into the packed ballroom, which was set up like a theater, with rows of chairs facing a small, elevated stage. Almost all the seats in the ballroom—and there must have been three hundred of them—were filled by eager reporters with flipped-open notebooks, digital voice recorders, or laptop computers. Video cameras mounted on tripods, halogen lamps already glaring, ringed the sea of seats, their lenses focused on the podium at the center of the stage beside a spindly rocking chair. Mr. Lemoncello was about to be tried in the press.

"Where's Irma?" asked Akimi as she, Kyle, and Angus slipped into the only empty seats they could find.

"Here she comes!" said Angus.

Kyle had to squirm a little to see above all the heads and shoulders in front of him. Finally he stood up.

"Down in front," growled a voice behind him. "You're blocking my shot."

Kyle crouched.

He could see two stately-looking old men in dark suits and bright white shirts escorting somebody's grandmother up the steps to the stage. She was dressed in a bell-shaped skirt so long it brushed along the floor. Her lace apron looked like a doily someone's grandmother might keep under her candy dish. Her powdery-white hair was tucked up into a bun.

"Dang," whispered Angus, "she really does look just like the Mrs. Maplebutter bottle."

Kyle agreed. "All she needs is the yellow plastic cap."

"Will you two knock it off?" said Akimi. "The Krinkles are about to speak."

The taller of the two businessmen stepped to the podium.

"Hello, everybody. Thank you for joining us. I'm David Krinkle. This is my brother, Frederick. As many of you know, we are the Krinkle brothers. We make games that make kids happy."

"No," whispered Kyle, "you make games that make kids sleepy."

"As game makers, we honor and respect the importance of ideas. Therefore, we were personally and professionally offended to hear that one of our so-called colleagues, Luigi Lemoncello, had blatantly stolen the idea for his first game—a major moneymaker—from this honest, hardworking entrepreneur, Irma Hirschman, who never received a dime after Mr. Lemoncello hijacked her intellectual property. By so doing, he has given our entire industry a black eye. How dare he steal this sweet little old lady's idea and call it his own?"

"Did you have a patent, Mrs. Hirschman?" shouted a reporter.

David Krinkle glared at the woman who dared ask such a rude question. "Have you no shame?" he said to her.

"That's okay," said the frail woman in a folksy Midwestern accent. She creaked up out of her rocking chair and dabbed at her damp eyes with a lacy handkerchief. "I'll answer the question."

She hobbled over to the podium.

"No, ma'am," she said, sniffling back her tears. "I don't have a patent, because on my stenographer's salary in 1969 I couldn't afford any fancy-pants patent attorneys. Besides,

I don't believe in patents. We wouldn't need a silly piece of paper if everybody just did what they know is right! Thou shalt not steal! Guess Mr. Lemoncello never made it to that chapter of the good book."

The crowd applauded.

"Do you have any proof that the young Luigi Lemoncello saw your game and copied it?" asked another reporter.

"Don't need it. Does he have any proof that he got his idea somewhere else? Of course not. If he did, why won't he show it to us?" Tears streaked down her face. "Mr. Lemoncello stole every single idea I had, right down to the game pieces—the boot, the cat, and the tiny harmonica. I read somewhere that Mr. Lemoncello *claims* he got the boot idea because some librarian gave him a 1972 knee-high Barbie doll boot in her desk drawer and let him borrow it while he worked on his game idea in her library. Ha! You believe that, folks, I've got a bridge in Brooklyn I'd like to sell you."

The audience tittered.

"The idea for that boot came from my mama, may she rest in peace. She just loved that Nancy Sinatra song about the boots and the walking. My mama is also the one who taught me about the American dream. If you work hard and play fair, you can do anything you want to do in this great country of ours. Even if it's just to make children happy."

Now the reporters were sniffling.

"Those buildings on the game board? You think the high and mighty Luigi Lemoncello sat down and whittled them all by himself, like I did? Heavens to Murgatroyd, why would he even bother? It was a whole heckuva lot easier just to steal 'em from me!"

Just about everybody in the audience shook their heads and grumbled in disgust.

But not Kyle and Angus. They dropped their jaws and gawked at each other.

"What?" said Akimi. "What'd she just say?"

Kyle told her: "The exact same thing the Mrs. Maplebutter bottle says in every single syrup commercial!"

37

The plane lifted off from Kansas City, headed for Ohio.

"'Heavens to Murgatroyd, that's mapley!' is what the Mrs. Maplebutter bottle says at the end of all the commercials," Kyle explained to Akimi and Abia.

"You mean what she *used* to say," added Angus. "I don't think there's been a Mrs. Maplebutter commercial on TV for maybe two years."

"You are correct," said Abia, who was already tapping keys on her banana jet computer. "Mrs. Maplebutter stopped making television commercials after the FDA informed Consolidated Corn Syrup Incorporated that it could no longer use the words 'mapley' or 'maplebutter,' since the only maple to be found in the product was trace elements of sawdust."

"So maybe the Krinkle brothers hired the same

actress," suggested Angus. "She's been out of work for a couple years. Probably needed the money."

"The Mrs. Maplebutter actress's real name is Beth Bennett," said Akimi, who was also clacking keys on her armrest computer. "She did the voice and posed for the bottle, which was animated with computer graphics."

She played a short video on the actress's website.

"*Heavens to Murgatroyd*," said the animated Mrs. Maplebutter bottle, "*that's mapley.*"

"She sounds just like Irma Hirschman!" exclaimed Abia.

"Are there any pictures of this actress?" asked Kyle.

"Yep," said Akimi, pivoting her screen so everybody could see the images she had uncovered. "Her most recent promo shot is in full Mrs. Maplebutter costume. I guess she did personal appearances at conventions and junk. Meet Beth Bennett, a.k.a. Irma Hirschman!"

"Those Krinkle brothers are so cheap," said Kyle. "They saved money by having her use her Mrs. Maplebutter costume to play Irma Hirschman."

"No wonder she was so good at crying on cue," said Angus. "She's an actress!"

Kyle plopped down in his swivel chair and fired up his computer.

"If she's an actress," he said, "I wonder what role she was playing in 1969."

As he tapped keys and entered search parameters, Kyle

suddenly had a new thought: Doing research was actually fun; sort of like being a super sleuth or master detective.

"Booyah!" he shouted when he found a particularly fascinating fact about Beth Bennett. "In 1969, Beth Bennett was in a show called *Put On Your Shoes* at the Melody Makers summer stock theater in Sheboygan, Wisconsin. Check out her head shot from the Playbill."

Kyle clicked on a thumbnail of a picture to make it fill his screen.

In her 1969 publicity shot, Beth Bennett had a bright smile, heavy black eye makeup, and blond hair that curled in to brush her apple cheeks.

"That's the exact same picture from the Family Frolic box top!" said Akimi excitedly. "We don't need her confession anymore. That's total proof that this whole thing is a hoax."

38

The four researchers grabbed a taxi at the airport.

"Do you kids have permission slips?" asked the cabbie.

"Yes!" said Akimi as the four players once again handed over their scrolled documents.

"Now drive like your pants are on fire!" said Abia.

"We need to tell Mr. Lemoncello the good news!" added Kyle.

The taxi took off but had to stop at a red light in the center of Alexandriaville. Kyle pressed his nose against the window as the car crept past the darkened library building. He could make out two police officers stationed on the shadowy steps.

"Here we go," said the cabbie. "Mr. Lemoncello's library."

"Fantastic," said Akimi. "But we want to go to Mr. Lemoncello's *house*."

"Hang on," said Angus. "Maybe we *should* stop here first."

"Good suggestion," said Abia. "We could retrieve the Family Frenzy patent as well as the shoebox with all the supporting materials."

"Um, hello?" said Akimi. "Those are cops guarding the front door."

"Maybe they'd let us in," said Angus.

"Really?" said Akimi. "In what parallel universe is that going to happen?"

"Take it easy, you guys," said Kyle. "We'll pick up the patent and stuff first thing tomorrow. The mayor has to reopen the library once he learns the truth."

"You want me to keep driving?" asked the cabbie.

"Yes, please," said Kyle. "Mr. Lemoncello's house."

"It used to be the Blue Jay Extended Stay Lodge," added Abia.

The cab pulled away from the curb. Kyle used his phone to call Miguel, who was with most of the other trustees at an ice cream parlor on Main Street. They were all drowning their sorrows in root beer floats.

"Tell everybody to meet us at Mr. Lemoncello's place."

"When?" asked Miguel.

"Now!"

"We're on our way!" said Miguel. "Mad Dog's with us. He'll bookmobile us over there in like three."

With Mad Dog at the wheel, the bookmobile beat the taxi to Mr. Lemoncello's mansion.

"What's up?" asked Miguel as he and six of the other contestants from the first two rounds of the Fabulous Fact-Finding Frenzy poured out of their boxy ride.

"I was right!" said Kyle. "Irma Hirschman is a fraud!"

"And we have proof," added Angus.

"Quite a lot of it," said Abia.

Kyle led the way up the front steps to Mr. Lemoncello's door and said, "Open sesame."

When they entered the foyer, yellow crime-scene police tape blocked the path to the living room.

"Kyle Keeley!" boomed Mr. Lemoncello. "My Fabulous Fact-Finding Frenziers! I can see all of you on my closed-circuit TV and, I must say, you're much more interesting than what's going on in the laundry room. No. Wait. Tiger Lily is using the litter box!"

"Um, how do we get where you are?" asked Kyle.

"Go through the secret panel."

Suddenly, the door to a giant grandfather clock swung open. The pendulum and weights rose like a stage curtain. The eleven data dashers stepped through the grandfather clock, strolled down a dimly lit passageway, and came out in the dining room, where Mr. Lemoncello stood with a man and a woman, both of whom had police badges dangling around their necks on lanyards.

"Welcome!" said Mr. Lemoncello. "I was going to hide my secret entrance inside a wardrobe, but C. S. Lewis beat me to it. Now then, what brings you here, besides of course a bookmobile and a taxicab?"

"Irma Hirschman is a phony!" blurted Akimi. "We have evidence!"

"Really?" said Mr. Lemoncello, heaving a giant sigh. "Too bad *they* don't."

He tilted his head toward the man and woman with the police badges.

"Mr. Lemoncello," said the man, "we got to be honest with you here. We're thinking this whole burglary report may be another one of your—what would you call it, Louise?"

"Another one of his lies," said his partner. "We know what you did to that sweet old grandma over in Missouri."

"She's an actress!" said Kyle.

"Right, kid. We saw her on TV. No actress could fake tears like that."

"You know," said Mr. Lemoncello, "I seldom watch TV. Except, of course, the Book Channel. And the Game Channel. And the Books About Games Channel." He glanced at his watch. "Oh, my. It's almost time for my favorite new show, *More Two-Letter Scrabble Words*."

He picked up the portable Nonfictionator and aimed it at a wall, which immediately turned into a ten-foot-wide TV screen.

A commercial filled the screen.

For a game.

From the Krinkle brothers.

A commercial that looked like it had been thrown together overnight.

"It's E-Float-E-Cons!" screamed an announcer. "It's just like charades but better, because it has hovering high-tech holograms!"

"Broadway shows!" screeched an actress pretending to be a kid.

Up popped the flat emoji:

"*Seven Brides for Seven Brothers*!" the actress shrieked, clapping her hands like a happy seal.

Bells dinged. Fireworks exploded. The commercial cut to a close-up of the E-Float-E-Cons box top.

"E-Float-E-Cons is a whole lot of holographic fun for the whole family," crooned the announcer. "And best of all, it's coming from the Krinkle brothers just in time for the holidays!"

"That's Mr. Lemoncello's idea!" Kyle shouted.

"No," said the lead detective, "it looks like the Krinkle brothers came up with it first."

"Those were the plans he showed us," said Elliott. "At dinner."

"Riiight," said the female detective.

"He did!" insisted Jamal. "He locked the blueprints in the floor safe."

"Then he told us all the combination!" added Pranav.

"Really?" said the top cop, still sounding skeptical. "My, what an interesting way to manage security for a multibillion-dollar corporation."

"They're my board of trustees, sir," said Mr. Lemoncello. "I trust them."

"You know what I trust? My gut. And my gut tells me you stole this E-Float-E-Cons game from the Krinkle brothers the same way you stole your first game from that nice lady in Utah."

"Missouri," his partner corrected him.

"Tomato, tahmahto."

"That 'nice lady' you're talking about is Mrs. Maplebutter!" Kyle practically screamed.

"I don't know about that, kid," said the detective, "but she sure is sweet."

"Fred?" said the female detective, making a face like she just smelled cat poop in the laundry room. "Let's get out of here. And, Mr. Lemoncello?"

"Yes?"

"Stick close to home. Irma Hirschman *and* the Krinkle brothers will want to know where to find you so they can sue you for every penny you've got!"

39

No one said anything for like five minutes after the two detectives left.

Finally, Mr. Lemoncello broke the silence.

"Soooo—have either of the two final teams brought back the fascinating fact about who or what was the inspiration for my very first board game?"

"No," admitted Akimi.

"We were going to look up the names of your brothers and sisters in the front of your family Bible," said Angus.

"But we sort of got sidetracked," said Kyle. "By the whole Family Frolic dealio."

"Of course," said Mr. Lemoncello. "You were doing research. You were duty bound to consider all the evidence uncovered. Would you final four fact finders like to request another delay of game?"

"Yes, sir," said Kyle. "We'd all rather spend our time

clearing your good name. Now, like we said, we can prove—"

Mr. Lemoncello held up his hand. Smiled faintly.

"If it's all right with you, Kyle, I'd rather spend *my* time reading a good book. Any suggestions, Sierra?"

"Well, sir, I like to read *Hatchet* by Gary Paulsen whenever I feel like I can't go on."

"Perfect. Help yourself to anything in the fridge or pantry, friends. I'll be in my reading room. Reading."

He stepped toward the door.

"You can't give up, Mr. Lemoncello," said Kyle.

"I know. In fact, I'm *not* giving up. However, I also cannot personally help you, as you say, 'clear my good name.' It would be like the Wicked Witch of the West saying, 'Hey, I'm not all that bad, Munchkins. Trust me.' No, Elphaba, the green-skinned girl who grew up to become that Wicked Witch, needed Gregory Maguire to write *Wicked* to clear her good name. I, on the other hand, need you."

"B-b-but . . ."

"Why do you think Dr. Zinchenko and I created a game that would send you children out into the field to find facts for our new exhibits that we ourselves had already found?"

"To make it fun for us to play?"

Mr. Lemoncello smiled. "Partially. But sometimes knowing how to find the answers and what questions to ask are more important than the answers themselves. With the research skills you twelve have honed in the Fabulous

Fact-Finding Frenzy, we hoped you would learn how to find facts on your own—facts that Dr. Zinchenko and myself did not already have."

Kyle nodded. "Like who's trying to make you look like a liar, a thief, and a cheat?"

"Exactly. I didn't know you'd be researching this particular subject right now, but that's why research skills are like tweezers. You just never know when you might need them. Now, if you will excuse me, there is nothing more that I personally can do except, of course, hope that our trust in our trustees was not misplaced."

Mr. Lemoncello clicked his heels together. His shoes burped. He bowed, twirled his fingers in front of his face, and exited the room.

Kyle and the others were on their own.

"Bummer," said Angus.

"Totally," agreed Pranav.

"Wait a second, you guys," said Elliott. "Where the heck is Katherine Kelly?"

"Probably over in her chalet," said Akimi. "Why?"

"She was my partner," said Elliott. "While we were driving around, she told me she's from Kansas City. Bragged about how it was the home of the best barbecue in America *and* the Krinkle Brothers game company."

"Yeah," said Kyle. "She mentioned that to me, too. When we first met."

"It's so obvious, we should've seen it sooner!" said

192

Elliott. "She's a spy! She planted that phony game box up in the Lemoncello-abilia Room. Then she stole the blueprints to the Fantabulous Floating Emoji game!"

"Katherine Kelly?" said Kyle. "No way."

"Way, dude," said Elliott. "I saw her write down the combination to the safe in her stupid little notebook when Mr. Lemoncello told it to us."

"Now that you mention it," said Sierra, "I saw her do that, too."

"She *is* from the Krinkle brothers' hometown," said Jamal.

"What more evidence do we need?" said Elliott.

"Please," said Abia, "I beg of you: Do not go there."

"Go where?" said Elliott, sounding defensive.

"Holding everybody in the state of Missouri responsible for the acts of two creepy old men."

"But it makes sense," said Diane.

"In the same way that it makes sense for the airport security screeners to give my father extra scrutiny every time he flies because his skin is brown and his first name is Muhammad?"

The room became quiet again.

"Abia's right," said Kyle. "Let's not jump to conclusions."

"Fine," said Elliott. "Whatever. Let's just go ask Katherine Kelly a few questions. Like Mr. Lemoncello said, we know how to find the truth!"

* * *

The eleven trustees went to Katherine Kelly's suite in a chalet located at the far edge of the old motel grounds.

She was in the one where the room and furniture were designed to look like snack cakes.

"Uh, hi, guys," said Katherine from the Hostess Twinkies sofa when everybody crowded into her living room. "What's up?"

"Why don't you tell us?" said Elliott, who probably watched a few too many lawyer shows on TV. "You're from Missouri. Kansas City, Missouri, to be precise. Just like the Krinkle brothers. Just like Irma Hirschman."

"Actually," said Akimi, "Ms. Hirschman is an actress from New York."

"Huh," said Katherine. "That's interesting. But why are you guys all here?"

"Because," said Elliott, "we think you may know something about who stole Mr. Lemoncello's game blueprints and gave them to the Krinkle brothers so they could steal Mr. Lemoncello's Fantabulous Floating Emoji idea."

Katherine Kelly turned a ghostly shade of puke-green.

"You're right. I think I do. And I feel totally responsible."

"Aha! Are you saying, Katherine Kelly, that *you* stole the blueprints?" demanded Elliott, hands clasped behind his back as if he were addressing the jury on the TV show *Law & Order.*

"What? No! No way. I would never steal anything from Mr. Lemoncello! Or give anything to the Krinkle brothers. I don't care where they live. Those two old guys are weird. And their games stink. I didn't do it."

"So why'd you turn green like that?" asked Akimi.

"Because," said Katherine, "I think I might've accidentally given the real thief the combination to the safe. We were in such a rush in the second leg of the race because we wanted to win that flight in Mr. Lemoncello's private jet."

"Awesome ride," said Angus.

"Excellent cookies," added Kyle. "Baked right on the plane."

"You're kidding," said Andrew. "You guys got free cookies?"

"Boys?" said Abia. "I believe Katherine was attempting to tell us how the floor-safe combination was stolen?"

"Right," said Kyle. "Our bad."

"We were in such a rush," said Katherine, "we left our backpack in the bookmobile. Remember, Elliott?"

"Vaguely."

"Well, I had dumped my notebook in that bag along with the clues and junk. Since I have trouble remembering stuff, I always write everything down."

"Even R-E-A-D?" said Elliott skeptically.

"Yes. Sorry. I have what they call 'working memory difficulties.' Anyway, the driver of our bookmobile in the second leg was a college girl named Jessica."

"We had her for the first leg," said Kyle. "Wait! When we came back from North Carolina, we saw her zipping up your backpack."

"She told us she wanted your sandwiches," added Abia.

"I think she wanted to steal more than our lunches," said Katherine. "I think she is the one working for the Krinkle brothers! I checked with Ms. Waintraub, the research librarian. She told me that Jessica quit her job and left town right after we all came back from North Carolina. Ms. Waintraub found it interesting that Jessica, a student at Alexandriaville State College, was originally from New York City but had booked a plane 'home' to Kansas City."

"Did she have a last name?" asked Abia.

"Yes. Bennett."

"*Whaaaaat?*" said Angus. "She's related to Mrs. Maplebutter?"

"It looms as a possibility," said Abia.

"A very large one," said Kyle. "Maybe the whole family is working for the Krinkle brothers."

Akimi tapped her lPad. "Found her Facebook page," she said. "Jessica Bennett. Two days ago she put up a post: 'Get ready for my grandmother's biggest starring role ever!' "

"Okay, okay," said Elliott. "I was wrong. Sorry, Katherine."

"That's okay," said Katherine. "She stole *your* sandwich, too."

Kyle and Akimi were selected to be the ones to tell Mr. Lemoncello the news. A robotic butler escorted them up to the second floor of the mansion and Mr. Lemoncello's reading room.

He was curled up on a floating beanbag chair, reading *Hatchet* by Gary Paulsen.

"Um, Mr. Lemoncello?" said Kyle.

"Just a minute," said Mr. Lemoncello, riveted by the pages of his novel. "I think this plane is about to crash."

"It's kind of important."

"So is a pilot who just had a heart attack!"

"We know who stole your game plans," blurted Akimi.

Mr. Lemoncello snapped the book shut. "I'm all ears, except for my nose and, of course, my eyes."

"It was one of the bookmobile drivers. Jessica Bennett."

"I see."

"We're pretty sure she's related to the actress pretending to be Irma Hirschman."

"My, what a felonious family."

"Jessica stole the combination out of Katherine Kelly's backpack during the second leg of the Fabulous Fact-Finding Frenzy," said Kyle.

"Then," said Akimi, "she drove over here while you were at the library, open-sesame'd your front door . . ."

"You really might want to consider a better security system out there, sir," suggested Kyle.

"Duly noted. Do go on, Miss Hughes."

"She waltzed into the dining room and found the floor safe—because Katherine was so afraid she might forget its location, she drew a diagram in her notebook."

"The same notebook Jessica found in the Wright brothers backpack," added Kyle.

"So," said Akimi, "Jessica grabbed the blueprints, dashed off to the airport in Cleveland, and grabbed the first flight she could to Kansas City—home of the Krinkle brothers."

Mr. Lemoncello nodded thoughtfully. "I suppose the Krinkle brothers were paying her more for stealing game ideas than I was giving her for driving a bookmobile. I know they paid Benjamin Bean a fortune."

"Who's Benjamin Bean?" asked Kyle.

"My first employee. I hired him right after Family Frenzy became such a huge, unexpected hit. I was going to follow it up with a sensationally fun picture-drawing version of charades that I called the Wondermous Whoop Dee Doodle game. If your team couldn't guess the answer from your sketches before the sand dial ran out, you had to sit on a whoopee cushion."

"Wait a second," said Akimi. "Don't the Krinkle brothers have a game called Whoop Dee Doodle?"

Mr. Lemoncello nodded. "It's their biggest hit. Has been for decades."

"And they stole it from you?" said Kyle.

"Yes. Stealing other people's ideas is, more or less, the Krinkle brothers' business model."

"Well," said Kyle. "You have to stop them or they'll keep on doing it."

Mr. Lemoncello grinned. "I already told you, I can't. No one would believe me or my lawyers. That's why I'm counting on you kids to do the research! You have all the training and skills you need. Now you simply need to trust yourself, trustees! Because I already do."

41

Walking down the steps from the reading room, Kyle realized things had gone from bad to worse to absolutely horrible.

The mayor had shut down the library.

The Krinkle brothers had smeared Mr. Lemoncello's good name and stolen his cool new holographic game idea.

The first law enforcement officers they had told about Irma Hirschman being a fraud had basically laughed in their faces because they were just kids.

And now Mr. Lemoncello was saying it was all up to Kyle and the others to find and reveal the truth.

No pressure or anything.

"What'd he say?" asked Miguel, who was waiting in Mr. Lemoncello's enormous dining room with the rest of the data dashers, including Katherine Kelly.

"Game over, thank you for playing," said Akimi.

"We've burned through our extra lives and are all out of quarters."

"Huh?" said Jamal. "Could you repeat that in English?"

"We're dead in the water," said Akimi.

"No, we're not," said Kyle. "We know the truth."

"And," said Miguel, "we also know nobody will listen to us. We're kids."

"Not to mention Mr. Lemoncello's biggest fans," added Katherine.

"Indeed," said Abia. "We hardly come across as unbiased researchers."

"It doesn't matter," said Kyle. "We just have to make the right moves. All games put you in a puzzle or a predicament. Then it's up to the players to figure out how to wiggle free."

"Very well," said Abia, "what do you suggest, Kyle Keeley?"

Kyle saw the Nonfictionator sitting on a table.

"I've got it!" he said. "Those detectives didn't believe us when we tried to tell them about Irma Hirschman being an actress. So we use this thing to dial up Abraham Lincoln again. Then, Honest Abe holds a press conference in a hotel ballroom, just like Irma Hirschman did, and tells everybody about the fake game box and the phony picture on it coming from a 1969 theatrical production in Sheboygan, Wisconsin. Then he tells them about Jessica stealing the blueprints. And since it's Honest Abe, everybody has to believe he's telling the truth!"

Eleven pairs of eyeballs were staring at Kyle.

"Seriously?" said Angus. "That's your plan?"

"It would look like a car commercial on Presidents' Day weekend," whined Andrew.

Abia was shaking her head. "I thought you were through looking for quick and easy solutions, Kyle Keeley. I am seriously disappointed to learn that this is not the case."

Kyle heard an annoying disco tune.

"That's my mother's ringtone!" said Andrew.

He pulled out his phone.

"Yes, Mother? No, we're at Mr. Lemoncello's. Seriously? Right now? Wow. Thank you, Mother." He ended the call. "Quick. Use that stupid remote thingy to turn on the stupid TV."

"Why?" asked Kyle, fumbling with the portable Nonfictionator.

"Because," said Andrew excitedly, "the Grand Gala is still on—minus Mr. Lemoncello, of course!"

Kyle bopped a red button and scrolled down the menu to "Dining Room TV." The white wall blinked and turned into a giant screen.

"This is Victoria Bartlett, Action News Eleven. We're here at the building formerly known as the Lemoncello Library, where world-famous game makers the Krinkle brothers have arrived to make an announcement about the Grand Gala, originally scheduled for tomorrow night. It was canceled, of course, due to the controversy swirling around Mr. Lemoncello and his reported theft of intellectual property. However, we're hearing that the canceled event may be back on. Wait. Here come the Krinkles. They are exiting their limousine and climbing up the front steps to the library."

"What are those guys doing here?" said Akimi.

"Is that Mrs. Chiltington?" said Miguel.

"Yes," said Andrew. "And Charles, too."

"And Mayor O'Brady," added Diane.

Kyle couldn't believe what he was seeing. Not the fact that the Chiltingtons had joined forces with the evil Krinkles and Mayor O'Brady. That was sort of to be expected. Birds of a feather always flocked together. Even vultures.

No, what Kyle couldn't believe was the guy standing behind the cluster of smiling dignitaries on the front steps of the library. The one very close to the keypad that could open the front bank vault door.

Mr. Raymo. Mr. Lemoncello's brand-new chief imagineer!

"The Krinkles are in place now," said the TV reporter. "Let's listen to what they have to say."

"Ladies and gentlemen, boys and girls," said David Krinkle while his brother, Frederick, smiled smugly. "My brother and I have generously volunteered to take over as entertainment directors here at your public library. As master game makers, we know how to make learning fun!"

"And," said the mayor, stepping forward, "the city of

Alexandriaville has graciously accepted their offer to serve in this capacity—free of charge!"

There was a smattering of applause. Mostly from Mrs. Chiltington's League of Concerned Library Lovers.

"We, the concerned citizens of Alexandriaville, are very, very pleased with this recent development," cooed Mrs. Chiltington operatically. "Very."

"Indubitably," added her son.

"With the help of Mr. Raymo," said David Krinkle, "who, by the way, is the real, uncelebrated genius behind all the marvels and magic inside this building, we will reopen tomorrow evening with a Grand Gala, when several new exhibits shall be revealed. We hope everybody in town will join us back here tomorrow at seven p.m. for a Krinkle Brothers extravaganza!"

That's when Frederick Krinkle stepped forward and smirked into the camera.

"My brother misspoke," he said. "Everyone in town is invited except, of course, for your local fraud, thief, and plagiarist, Luigi L. Lemoncello!"

42

"Unbelievable," said Akimi, shaking her head at the TV screen. "The Krinkle brothers are taking over the library, and Mr. Raymo's gone over to the dark side."

Kyle watched Mr. Raymo tap the electronic keypad next to the bank vault door. Ten seconds later, it swung open. The Krinkle brothers stepped into the circular doorway with Mr. Raymo. The Chiltingtons wanted to go with them, as did the mayor, but the taller brother, David, held up his hand like a traffic cop.

"We have work to do inside, good people of Alexandriaville," he announced. "You are all invited back tomorrow evening. Come along, Mr. Raymo."

The three figures disappeared and, with a heavy *thunk* of the bank vault door, locked themselves inside.

Kyle shook his head and shut off the TV.

"That's it," said Kyle. "They win."

"What?" asked Angus. "Why?"

"No way can we get into the library now. We should've grabbed the patent and that old shoebox last night like you guys said. We could've shown the world the Barbie boot and models that Irma Hirschman swore Mr. Lemoncello didn't have!"

Abia nodded. "Yes. It would have been excellent primary-source research materials."

"Um, hello?" said Akimi. "There were police guarding the front door, remember?"

"Well," said Abia, "perhaps we should return to the library. I have found that sometimes, in the quest for knowledge, you must go backward before you can move forward."

"I guess that's why they call it research," said Andrew. "Sometimes you have to re-*search* for things you might've missed the first time you searched."

"Riiiight," said Akimi, rolling her eyes. "That's why they call it that."

"Okay, here's our big problem," said Kyle. "I mean besides getting past the cops into the locked library, of course. Where exactly in the library did Mr. Lemoncello store that shoebox?"

"Easy answer," said Akimi.

"Where?"

"Upstairs."

"In the Dewey decimal rooms?"

"No, I mean Mr. Lemoncello is upstairs. Why don't we just go up there and ask him?"

When Kyle and Akimi returned to the second-floor reading room, Mr. Lemoncello had his nose buried in a new book—*Unstoppable,* a football story by Tim Green.

"The kids in this gripping gridiron saga never give up," said Mr. Lemoncello. "Very inspirational."

"We won't give up, either," said Kyle. "But we need to know where you stored your backup material for your very first patent. The one for Family Frenzy."

"In the library."

"Is it in the Art and Artifacts Room?" asked Akimi.

"Oh, no. That would be far too showy."

"So it's in the Lemoncello-abilia Room?"

"Oh, no. Too pretentious. You see, friends, I am a modest man. That's why I did not want a holographic exhibit about me until Dr. Zinchenko's mother insisted. The patent and all its supporting paraphernalia are downstairs. In the basement. In the stacks."

"Do you know where?" asked Kyle.

"Yes. The shoebox is in a carton. A cardboard carton."

"Can you be a little *more* vague?" cracked Akimi.

"You're right. I should be better organized. You might ask Miguel or Andrew. They moved a lot of those old cartons around a couple weeks ago—all the papers from my early years in the game-making game. Back when the Imagination Factory wasn't even a full-fledged idea. It was more of an inkling, which, by the way, is not a small pen."

"Okay," said Kyle, "we'll be back."

"Where are you going?"

"To sneak into your library!"

"I see. Do you have a permission slip?"

"Nope. But we're going to do it anyway!"

"Oh-kay," Akimi said to Kyle. "Now you've completely flipped your lid. We're going to go all ninja-slash–*Mission: Impossible* and break into the heavily guarded library building?"

"We have to," said Kyle. "This is the real race. We have to go back to the library, find the proof we need, and show it to the world before the Krinkle brothers find it and destroy it!"

"Might I offer a suggestion?" said Mr. Lemoncello.

"Only if it's 'quit,' " said Akimi.

"Oh, no. If you quit once, it becomes a habit. Never quit! My new chum Michael Jordan taught me that."

"What's the suggestion?" asked Kyle.

"While you're down in the basement, you might also look for a box labeled 'The Benjamin Bean Affair.' I never pressed any charges against the Krinkle brothers, even though Max, my lawyer, said we had more than enough evidence. The contents of that particular carton might prove extremely embarrassing to the Krinkle brothers."

"It might also show the world who the real thieves and plagiarists are," said Kyle, his competitive drive kicking into gear big-time.

"Oh, that would be wondermous," said Mr. Lemoncello. "It would also be hazardific. The getting-back-into-the-library part, I mean. I feel quite certain Mayor O'Brady has beefed up security."

"I don't care," said Kyle. "The truth is the truth, and people need to know it."

"But how *are* we going to get into the library?" asked Akimi. "One of those deals where we drop through a sky-light in a zip-line harness?"

Kyle shook his head. "No need. Mr. Lemoncello already gave us the combination to the front door. The same one he uses for everything: R-E-A-D!"

"Actually," said Mr. Lemoncello, "Mr. Raymo changed that lock."

Once again, Kyle and Akimi were gobsmacked.

"You don't know how to open your own front door?" said Kyle.

"No. Not anymore. You see, once we installed the Nonfictionator, Mr. Raymo insisted that he take over major security issues such as front door lock combinations. As you two have pointed out, I tend to be a little lax in that department."

"But Mr. Raymo is working for the Krinkle brothers!"

Mr. Lemoncello arched a bushy eyebrow. "Kyle Keeley, must you always jump to conclusions?"

"You mean he isn't?" said Kyle.

"What I mean is, like all of us, Mr. Raymo is innocent until *proven* guilty."

"He walked into the building with those oily Krinkle brothers," said Akimi, throwing up her arms in exasperation. "What more proof do you need?"

"More than that," said Mr. Lemoncello. "Who's to say Mr. Raymo isn't one of my most loyal employees and that he volunteered to risk his life, fortune, and sacred honor to go undercover and keep an eye on the nefarious Krinkle brothers for me?"

"Seriously?" said Kyle. "He's still a good guy?"

"One of the best," said Mr. Lemoncello proudly. "He may be new to the library, but he has worked for me in New York City for three decades!"

"Would he let us in?" asked Akimi.

"Undoubtedly."

"Then what are we waiting for?" said Kyle. "Come on, Akimi. We need to find out where Andrew and Miguel stored those cartons!"

44

"You guys?" Kyle said to all the others assembled in Mr. Lemoncello's dining room. "We need to head back to the library and find that shoebox."

"Plus some other very important papers," added Akimi.

"You better do it soon," said Elliott, gesturing toward the TV wall. The sound was muted, but Kyle could read the headlines: "Mayor O'Brady Suggests Renaming Former 'Lemoncello' Library After His Wife, Bernice. People in Bowling Green, Ohio, Laugh at the Suggestion."

"We're doing it tonight," said Kyle. "Where's Andrew?"

"He went home," said Sierra. "He said he needed time to figure out what to wear at the gala tomorrow."

"Okay, then it's up to you, Miguel."

"Yo, that's cool. What do I need to do?"

"Help us find those cartons you and Andrew moved

around in the stacks a couple weeks ago. The ones about the early years at the Imagination Factory."

"No problem. I remember where we put them. Kind of. Well, you know, sort of. There were a lot of boxes to reorganize."

"Just do your best," said Sierra.

"Angus?" said Kyle. "Are you in?"

"Sure. What do I need to do?"

"Probably something wild and crazy and dangerous," said Akimi.

"Awesome."

"I would like to go as well," said Abia.

"Great," said Kyle. "Because I was just about to ask you to join the team. When it comes to doing research and finding junk, you're the best."

"Thank you, Kyle Keeley."

"We might need some research in Kansas City, too."

"I can handle that," said Katherine. "After all, it's my hometown."

"Great," said Kyle. "We'll have Mr. Lemoncello's corporate jet fly you and Elliott out there. Be sure you both bring your permission slips. And tell your parents where you're going."

"Um, we should probably do the same thing," said Akimi.

"Already did," said Kyle. "Sent them a text saying Mr. Lemoncello was feeling blue so we're all watching *The Sound of Music* with him."

"Seriously?"

"Hey," said Kyle, "whiskers on kittens can cheer up anybody! You guys might want to text the same thing."

Akimi, Miguel, Angus, Abia, Elliott, and Katherine all shrugged, then thumbed their phones.

Kyle turned to Katherine and Elliott. "While you're in Missouri, see if you can grab a video interview with an actress named Beth Bennett. You already know her grand-daughter Jessica."

"We'll tell this Bennett dame that we know the truth," said Elliott, still sounding like a TV detective. "Maybe that'll make her spill the beans!"

"Beth Bennett is an actress," said Katherine. "She'll *loooove* being in front of a camera again. Don't worry. She'll talk."

"Awesome," said Kyle. "Send any media files to my phone."

"You got it!"

"What about the rest of us?" asked Jamal Davis. "We want to help, too."

"I know," said Kyle. "But if too many of us try to sneak into the building tonight, they'll catch us for sure."

"And," added Akimi, "if we're busted, you guys need to be plan B."

"Cool," said Pranav. "And what will be plan B?"

"Something besides what we just tried," said Kyle. "Because if we need you to go to plan B, that means plan A totally tanked."

Pranav nodded. "We'll be standing by."

"Is Mad Dog still outside?" asked Kyle.

"Yeah," said Jamal, peering out a window. "His bookmobile is parked in the driveway."

"Perfect. We have our ride back to the library."

"That's not going to be too stealthy," said Miguel. "A big honking bookmobile driving up to the library when everybody knows the place is closed."

"Mad Dog can tell whoever asks that he came back because he needed a new load of books. While he's doing that, we'll sneak up to the front door."

"And how are you guys going to open it?" asked Katherine. "Do you know the combination?"

"No, but Mr. Raymo will help us with that," said Kyle. "We hope."

"He's still one of the good guys," added Akimi. "In fact, he's one of Mr. Lemoncello's most loyal employees. He's just pretending to work for the Krinkle brothers."

"That is so nice," said Sierra.

"Here are some flashlights I found in the kitchen pantry," said Diane Capriola, floating back into the room in Mr. Lemoncello's drone slippers. "They were on one of the highest shelves. Figured you guys might need them."

Kyle's eyes were focused on the floating footwear. "We might need *those,* too," he said.

"For what?" asked Diane.

"I don't know. We're kind of making this up as we go."

The flashlights and slippers went into the bright yellow

backpack Kyle and Abia used during the last leg of the Fabulous Fact-Finding Frenzy. Kyle looked around the dining room. He saw the portable Nonfictionator sitting on a table.

"We'll take this, too."

"Why?" asked Akimi.

"It's a universal remote. Maybe it will work like a garage door opener on the bank vault lock."

"Seriously?"

"It's worth a try."

"Fine. Whatever. We need to hurry. The longer the Krinkle brothers are alone in the library, the more damage they can do."

"They're probably looking for the exact same evidence," said Sierra. "If they find it first . . ."

Kyle nodded. Sierra was right.

If the Krinkles found Mr. Lemoncello's patent and Family Frenzy shoebox before the undercover research team did, they'd probably toss it all into the trash!

Or burn it!

45

"Far out," was all Mad Dog said when Kyle told him why he and the four others needed a ride to the library at nine o'clock at night.

When the bookmobile was two blocks away from the library, Mad Dog doused the headlights and shut off the engine.

"We are now operating in what I like to call the silent-but-deadly mode," he whispered to everybody huddled in the back as the vehicle quietly coasted down the block.

"Cool," said Miguel.

"Uh-oh."

"What?" said Kyle.

"Couple heavies guarding the front door," whispered Mad Dog. "No dreadlocks. That means it's not my buds Clarence and Clement."

"Probably those same cops," said Angus.

"No, they look more like private security goons," reported Mad Dog from the front seat, where he was waving and smiling. "They're wearing navy-blue blazers and gray slacks. Cops don't wear matching sport coats, man."

Kyle's heart was racing.

This whole plan might be over before it even starts.

"Angus?" he said. "Are you ready to do something dangerous and crazy?"

"Always. Lay it on me."

The bookmobile came to a stop.

"Uh-oh," said Mad Dog from behind the wheel. "The hired muscle is walking this way. I must've parked where I'm not supposed to park."

"Okay, Angus," said Kyle. "Slip out the back door. Hide behind that giant oak tree. When the guards start talking to Mad Dog—"

"We'll make all sorts of noise and run around to the back of the building," finished Akimi.

"What do you mean 'we'?" asked Angus.

"We're a team. The two of us can cause a bigger distraction."

"Cool."

"When the guards chase after you guys," said Kyle, "Abia, Miguel, and I'll hightail it to the front door."

"If they chase us around the block," said Akimi, "we can probably buy you guys like five minutes."

"If Mr. Raymo helps us, five minutes should be all we need."

"Go, you guys," said Mad Dog. "They're halfway here."

"Crank up your engine," Kyle told Mad Dog. He turned to Akimi and Angus. "If you guys are in the lead when you circle back, jump into the bookmobile and take off."

"What?" said Akimi. "How will you guys get home?"

"I'm hoping Mr. Raymo will give us a lift. Hurry. Go!"

Akimi and Angus slipped out the rear emergency exit.

Kyle put on the heavy backpack, grabbed the handle for the side door, and crouched beside it. Abia and Miguel crouched behind him. Kyle would wait to pop open the door until the guards were chasing after Angus and Akimi.

"Hey there, dudes," Mad Dog said to someone at the passenger-side window of the boxy bookmobile. "Whazzup?"

"What are you doing here?" asked one of the guards.

"Needed some new books," said Mad Dog, jabbing his thumb over his shoulder. "We usually reload after nine o'clock every night."

"Not tonight," said the guard.

"But—"

"Not tonight. The library is under new management."

"But Mr. Lemoncello—"

"Mr. Lemoncello ain't running things no more. Now move this vehicle."

"The Krinkle brothers need this parking spot to unload a truck full of games they're going to sell at the gala tomorrow night," said a second guard.

219

"Cool," said Mad Dog, buying time for Angus and Akimi to set up their diversion. "Are the games good?"

"Nah. They're crummy, but they're cheap. I buy 'em for my nieces and—"

"Come on," Kyle heard Akimi holler. "I know where there's a secret tunnel into the library!"

"Hey, you kids!" shouted the guard. "Where do you think you're going?"

"Oh, no!" shouted Angus. "Run! They might catch us!"

"Hey! You two! Come back here!"

The first guard took off running.

"Move this vehicle!" shouted the second guard as he joined in the pursuit.

Mad Dog checked the side-view mirrors. "Okay. They're running up the street. Akimi and Angus are in the lead. They're rounding the corner. The guards are so out of shape, man, they can barely jog. Go! The goons just took the corner!"

Kyle yanked open the side door. Hunkered down, he flew to the front steps of the library. He could hear Abia and Miguel running right behind him. They bounded up the three tiers of marble and faced the bank vault door.

Kyle rapped his fist against the steel-clad concrete.

It hurt his knuckles.

"Mr. Raymo? It's Kyle Keeley. Mr. Lemoncello sent us! Let us in!"

He waved at a security camera.

Nothing.

"Mr. Raymo?" He pounded the door.

Still nothing.

"So," whispered Miguel, "is this when we call Jamal and the gang and tell them to initiate plan B?"

"Not yet."

Kyle stared at the keypad mounted on the wall beside the circular door. It was set up like a telephone but with just numbers, no letters.

Of course, that didn't really matter.

Because, just like Mr. Lemoncello, Kyle had no clue what the combination might be.

46

"I need numbers," Kyle muttered, as much to himself as to Abia and Miguel.

"What numbers?" said Abia.

"I don't know!"

"Kyle?" said Miguel. "We've been buds since like first grade but I got to tell you, this is the most backward game plan you've ever come up with."

"That's it!" said Kyle. "Backward. Maybe Mr. Raymo used backward logic. Told Mr. Lemoncello he didn't use R-E-A-D because he actually did!"

"Um, okay," said Miguel. "I guess . . ."

"Seven-three-two-three!" shouted Abia. "Those are the alphanumeric positions for R-E-A-D on a telephone keypad."

Kyle tapped in the numbers.

The keypad flashed red.

The words "false entry" scrolled across an LED window followed by "after two more false tries alarm will sound."

Great.

"Wait a second," said Miguel. "What about 'open sesame,' like on his front door at home?"

"What's that in numbers?" said Kyle.

"Uh, um, er . . . ," stammered Miguel, staring at the keypad.

"6-7-3-6, 7-3-7-2-6-3!" said Abia.

Kyle tapped it in. The red warning lights flashed again. The LED scroll warned that he had one more try.

"You'll never catch us!" they heard Angus shout from somewhere not too far away.

"We better head back to the bookmobile," said Abia.

"No," said Kyle. "We have one more shot."

"But if you are wrong, the alarms will sound!"

"I know."

Kyle closed his eyes. Concentrated. Mr. Lemoncello always used R-E-A-D. Mr. Raymo changed it, though.

"Open sesame" was backward at his mansion. So was the scratched code on the fence outside his childhood home.

Could it be that simple?

It was worth a try.

He put his fingers on the keypad.

"Yo, bro," said Miguel. "Be ready to run if you're wrong."

"I will," said Kyle.

Kyle tapped 3-2-3-7 on the keyboard—the numbers for R-E-A-D if you spelled it backward.

He heard a whirr, a clank, and a *KERTHUNK*.

The front door *whoosh*ed open.

"Come on!" Kyle, Abia, and Miguel leapt inside and shouldered the vault door shut.

They heard tires squealing.

The bookmobile had just taken off—hopefully with Akimi and Angus inside.

"We're in," said Kyle, his heart pounding.

He took a deep breath.

The library lobby was eerily dark and quiet. Someone had switched off Mr. Lemoncello's trickling fountain. The only illumination came from sporadic security lights mounted on the walls.

"Let's head down to the basement," whispered Kyle. "But no flashlights until we're safe in the stacks."

The trio tiptoed into the Rotunda Reading Room, which was already being set up for the Grand Gala the next night.

"They're using the same new exhibits," said Miguel.

Ghostly green hologram grids for Thomas Edison, Emily Dickinson, Michael Jordan, the Wright brothers, and Abraham Lincoln were arrayed around the floor of the rotunda like figures in a wax museum.

The holographic Mr. Lemoncello was there, too, but he wasn't alone. That Supreme Court justice, Oliver Wendell Holmes Jr., was posed next to him, sitting behind an elevated judge's bench, a gavel poised in his hand.

"My guess," said Abia, "is they have programmed the three-D Lemoncello image to make some sort of public confession tomorrow night during the gala."

She was probably right. The stiff Mr. Lemoncello was holding a board game in his hands as if it were a cafeteria tray. "Family Frolic by Irma Hirschman" was printed boldly across the box top. *This is so unfair,* thought Kyle. He knew the good guys didn't always win. But he was going to make sure Mr. Lemoncello at least had a fighting chance!

"This way, you guys," whispered Miguel. "Andrew and I took these steps over—"

He stopped talking when they saw the silhouette of a short, shadowy, bald-headed figure scurry into the room.

Mr. Raymo.

"Hello?" he said, squinting into the darkness. "Is anybody here?"

Kyle snapped on his flashlight. Waved.

"Good!" said Mr. Raymo in a hushed voice. "You were able to crack my rudimentary code."

Suddenly, they heard footsteps clomping down one of the spiral staircases.

"Quick," said Mr. Raymo. "Hide! It's the Krinkles!"

"Under the tables, guys," said Kyle, snapping off his flashlight.

Kyle ducked under one of the reading tables. Abia and Miguel followed his lead—each one hiding beneath a different table to increase the odds of at least one of them not getting caught.

"There you are," Kyle heard one of the Krinkle brothers, the grumpier one, Frederick, say. "The shoebox wasn't in the Lemoncello-abilia Room."

"Which," said the other brother, David, "we need to padlock before tomorrow night."

"On it," said Mr. Raymo, tapping on his tablet computer, playing along.

"We'll continue the search for Luigi's legendary shoebox later," said Frederick. "Right now we need to locate whatever other new game ideas he's been dreaming up, so we can send them along to our design department and watch them become brand-new Krinkle Brothers games!"

What? Kyle fumed to himself. No way was he going to let that happen. The Krinkles would take all of Mr. Lemoncello's brilliant ideas and make them stinkle!

"Where's Luigi's office, Chet?" demanded David.

Mr. Raymo led the Krinkle brothers back to the fiction wall and opened the secret bookcase panel. The second the

226

hidden door swung shut, Kyle, Abia, and Miguel scrambled out of their hiding places.

"Okay, Miguel," said Kyle. "Mr. Raymo just bought us some time. Take us to that shoebox."

"Follow me."

They scampered across the marble floor to the staircase that led down to the basement and the stacks—the place where the library stored its collection of research materials that couldn't be checked out but only used in the building.

"I hope I can remember where we put that stuff," said Miguel nervously.

Kyle hoped he could, too.

47

Switching on their flashlights, Kyle, Abia, and Miguel made their way down the steps into the library's cavernous basement.

In the dim light, Kyle could see that the very long, very wide cellar was just as he remembered it: filled with tidy rows of floor-to-ceiling shelving units, all of them jam-packed with cardboard cartons.

"I hope the shelves don't start attacking you again," joked Miguel.

When Kyle had come down to the stacks searching for a clue in the escape game, the walls of heavy metal bookcases automatically slid and skated around, forming a moving maze that nearly crushed him.

"Me too," said Kyle.

The shelving units were individually labeled with red

LED signs that glowed in the dark like cat eyes. They were in a section filled with magazines from the 1940s.

"We put the boxes with stuff from Mr. Lemoncello's early business career on a shelf labeled 'The Imagination Factory/Year One.'"

"So where is it?" asked Kyle.

"I remember it was pretty close to the book-sorting machine," said Miguel. "I think."

"Great," said Kyle. "Lead the way."

Miguel headed up one wall of shelves, turned down an alleyway where that wall ended, turned left, then right, then right again, and right one more time. A shadow flickered across the wall.

"What was that?" gasped Miguel.

"My flashlight," said Kyle.

"Don't do that, man!"

"You have no idea where you put those boxes, do you, Miguel Fernandez?" demanded Abia after they ended up back where they had started.

"The lights were on when we did it," said Miguel.

"Think, Miguel," said Kyle. "This is really, really important."

"I'm sorry. But when Andrew and I were organizing the boxes, we just basically loaded up the robots and followed them to the right spot."

"The robots!" said Kyle.

The Lemoncello Library employed an army of robotic,

computerized book carts that crawled around on tank treads through the stacks finding requested research material.

Kyle dug the Nonfictionator out of his backpack and scrolled through the options for the universal remote.

"Robotic Research Assistant" was listed right after "Refrigerator."

Kyle thumbed the robot icon.

With the hum of an electric motor and a *whoosh* of hydraulics, a robotic cart with blinking green headlights scooted up the aisle. It stopped at Kyle's feet and just sat there. Blinking at him.

"Now what?" said Abia.

"You have to tell it what you're looking for," said Miguel, stepping forward. "Hello, Researchio."

The robot scanned Miguel's face with its green lasers.

"That's its facial recognition software kicking in," he explained. "Andrew and I were prescreened to use the robots so we wouldn't have to go upstairs to the reference desk every time we wanted to move a box."

"Welcome back, MIGUEL FERNANDEZ," blurped the robot. "How may I be of research assistance today?"

"We're looking for Luigi Lemoncello's original patent and accompanying materials for the board game titled Family Frenzy."

"One moment," said the robot. "One moment. Searching. Searching. I have an original patent document and accompanying materials for a board game titled Family

Frenzy in section twelve. Is that what you are searching for, MIGUEL FERNANDEZ?"

"Yes," said Abia. "That is precisely what he asked you to find."

"Yo, Abia, ease up," said Miguel. "He's a robot. That's just how they programmed him."

"Sorry," said Abia. "My bad."

"You are forgiven," said the robot. "Please. Follow me."

The robot beeped a few times, twirled to the right, and rumbled down a sideways corridor between bookshelves.

"Way to go, Miguel!" said Kyle. "This is actually going to work!"

48

"Everything should be in that box on the top shelf!" said Miguel as the robot rose up on its extendable scissor-lift legs.

The towering shelf was gigantic—maybe twenty-five feet tall.

"Retrieving carton," chirped the robot.

Its folding supports opened in a crisscross X pattern that vertically elevated the box-grabbing apparatus closer to the ceiling.

"This is so awesome," said Miguel.

But then the robot stuttered to a stop.

It was five feet short of the shelf.

"Maximum height limit has been achieved," it peeped. "Contacting control center for alternate, taller, big-boy robotic research assistant."

"No!" said Kyle as loudly as he could while still whispering.

"No!" Miguel said to the robot.

The bot blinked. "Awaiting further instructions."

"Kyle?" said Abia. "Why won't you let the robot summon assistance?"

"Because if it contacts the control center, lights are going to start flashing upstairs. In the control room. On Mr. Raymo's tablet computer. Maybe even in Mr. Lemoncello's office."

"And the bad guys will know someone is down here in the basement!" said Miguel. "Good catch, Kyle."

"Thanks."

"So what are we going to do now?" said Abia, leaning back to examine the top shelf. She swung her flashlight across the crate.

Squinting, Kyle could read the markings on the outside of the box. It was clearly the one they needed. But it was perched at the tippy-top of a metal shelving unit towering unsteadily over them.

Kyle grabbed the nearest shelf. Gave it a short shove.

The whole thing wobbled.

"I am not able to climb up there to retrieve it," reported Abia.

"Me neither," said Miguel. "I'm afraid of heights."

"I'm not," said Kyle, dipping into the backpack again. This time, he pulled out Mr. Lemoncello's drone slippers.

"Do you know how to use those devices?" asked Abia.

"Sure. They're slippers. You slip them on your feet."

Kyle sat on the floor and yanked off his tennis shoes.

"You could crash and injure yourself!" said Abia when Kyle stood up, his feet snug in the fuzzy slippers.

"I'm not going to injure anything," said Kyle. "I'm just going to float up there and grab a box."

He stomped on his heels.

Nothing happened.

He went up on tippy toe.

Nothing.

"Do like in *The Wizard of Oz*," suggested Miguel.

"Huh?"

"All you have to do is knock the heels together three times and command the shoes to carry you wherever you wish to go!"

Kyle shrugged. It was worth a try.

He clicked his heels together three times and said, "Up there. That, uh, shelf."

He felt a tingle in his toes and a tickle under the soles of his feet. As the drone propellers started spinning, there was a soft *BRRRRR*, like that of an electric toothbrush. Three seconds later, he rose off the floor.

He was floating in front of the rickety shelving unit. It was a slow ascent but absolutely amazing. Pretty soon he was higher than the stalled robot. A minute later, he was level with the cardboard carton labeled "Family Frenzy: Diagrams, Mock-up, and Patent."

"Grab the box," coached Miguel.

Kyle leaned forward.

"Whoa . . ."

And nearly lost his balance.

After flapping his arms to steady himself, he tried again.

This time he grabbed the carton.

"Dump it in that wire basket dealio on the robot!" cried Miguel.

"Good idea," said Kyle, still wobbly with the extra weight of the box in his arms. "Uh, any idea how I get down?"

Miguel and Abia answered together: "Knock your heels together. . . ."

"Riiiight. Three times." He clicked his heels again. "Take me down, please."

Kyle slowly drifted down and placed the cardboard container in the robot's basket.

"Uh, now take me all the way down to the floor," Kyle said to his slippers after knocking the heels together three more times.

"Lower box!" Miguel said to the robot.

The robot did as instructed.

Abia lifted the lid.

"It is the patent and shoebox," she declared. "Everything we need is in here. Mr. Lemoncello's original mockup with all the tokens he either whittled or borrowed from his librarian friend, Mrs. Gail Tobin. Here's the Barbie doll go-go boot and the tiny harmonica and the cat charm from the librarian's bracelet."

"Excellent," said Kyle.

"This is exactly what we need," added Miguel. "Nothing stops a lie faster than cold hard facts."

"So let's go dig up some more," said Kyle.

"You got it, bro." Miguel turned to the robot. "Researchio? Go find me everything you can about the Benjamin Bean affair!"

49

"Must be right near here," said Kyle as the robot skidded sideways about two yards.

"Makes sense," said Abia. "We are dealing with the same time period, the early 1970s. Benjamin Bean stole Mr. Lemoncello's whoopee-cushion-doodle idea for the Krinkle brothers right after Family Frenzy became his first surprise hit."

"The record you seek is on the third shelf," said the robot.

"Awesome," said Kyle.

The robot lengthened its forklift arms.

Into an empty space.

"There is nothing there," said Abia.

"The material you just requested has already been requested by another patron," said the robot in an entirely different voice.

"That sounds like the reference librarian," said Abia. "Ms. Waintraub."

Researchio's head rotated and one of his green LED headlamps flickered as it turned into a holographic projector. A shorter version of the research librarian, maybe two feet tall, appeared on the floor in front of Kyle, Abia, and Miguel.

"What's going on here?" Kyle demanded.

Abia propped her hands on her hips and bent down as if she were scolding a garden gnome. "We need that other box! The one about Benjamin Bean. Quit being obstinate, Ms. Adrienne Waintraub!"

"I'm sorry," said the hologram in her matter-of-fact way. "As I stated previously, the material you requested has already been checked out by another patron. There are no other copies of the materials you seek anywhere in this library or, for that matter, the known universe. Kindly request it again at a later date."

"Oh, man," said Miguel. "This is why I like real librarians. They're search engines with a heart. This one's just a machine!"

"You forgot to mention how much more efficient I am," replied the hologram.

"Who took the box?" Kyle asked the holographic librarian.

"I am not at liberty to divulge that information."

"When did they request it?" demanded Abia.

"It is due back in twenty-three hours and fifty-five minutes."

"There's a one-day research limit on stack items," said Miguel.

"That means it was just checked out five minutes ago!" said Abia.

"Correct," said Ms. Waintraub with a very un-holographic wink.

"The Krinkle brothers!"

Miguel spun around and shone his flashlight up toward the ceiling, illuminating the tracks of the bin transport system.

"This is a new contraption Mr. Raymo installed a couple weeks ago," said Miguel. "The robots place the requested cartons into one of the big blue bins over there. A chain between the tracks hauls the bins up the wall. Then they shuttle along the rails like cars on a roller coaster, disappear through that hole, and eventually pop up right underneath the reference desk."

"There," said Kyle, pointing his flashlight at a cardboard box slowly rising up the wall. It was tucked into a bright blue plastic bin, which was being towed by a thick chain set between two tubular tracks. There were empty blue bins crawling up the wall, every three feet, right behind it.

It was so close.

There was no way Kyle was going to let the Krinkle brothers get their hands on it before he did.

"Hurry," said Abia. "If we take the stairs, we might be able to intercept the carton the instant it appears underneath the reference desk."

"Wait," said Kyle. "There's a faster way. Those bins look big enough to sit in!"

"True," said Miguel. "Because some of the cartons down here are humongous."

Kyle dashed over to the wall in his drone slippers.

"What are you doing now, Kyle Keeley?" cried Abia.

"Going on a quick roller-coaster ride! Meet me upstairs, you guys, under the reference desk. Bring the shoebox. And my sneakers, too!"

Kyle clicked his heels together three times.

"Take me up to the blue bin right below that brown box!"

He floated up the wall, swung around, and plopped his butt into a bin already climbing the incline.

When the conveyor belt finished its ascent, the bin tilted backward. Kyle felt like an upside-down turtle in a blue plastic shell. He wiggled around and forced himself into a sitting position, his head barely missing the ceiling by about two inches.

He could see the carton he needed riding along in the bin right in front of his.

He tried to lean forward, reach out, and grab it. But it was too far away.

That's when he saw the big drop.

It became clear to Kyle pretty quickly that the library basement was divided into two sections.

And he was about to plunge into the second one!

He tipped forward as his bin entered a black hole and streaked downhill in a nearly ninety-degree angle, rumbling into whatever the darkness was hiding on the other side of the dividing wall. He gripped the hard plastic sides of his roller-coaster car so tightly his fingers hurt.

Since there was absolutely no light, Kyle couldn't see what was coming next.

But he could sure feel it.

First he was slammed sideways in a sharp turn to the right. Then he was slammed back in an even sharper turn to the left.

After two more rib-crunching twists and turns, his

stomach leapt up and down in his throat as he careened across a series of rolling hills.

And then there was another vertical drop. A free fall! To make things worse, the blue bins weren't equipped with seat belts—because people weren't supposed to ride in them, just boxes!

Just when he thought the g-forces might stretch his cheeks into his ears, the roller coaster slammed on its brakes. Kyle nearly flew out of the box.

But the bin had finally stopped moving.

And he was still alive.

Kyle started breathing again.

Until he heard a chain clinking.

His bin tilted backward. Again!

He was climbing straight up another twenty-foot wall, his head bouncing and banging against the lip of the plastic box.

This was such a bad idea, he thought. *Bad, bad, bad, bad, bad.*

Kyle realized he couldn't help Mr. Lemoncello all that much if he ended up dead.

Finally he saw a small window of light that grew wider as the bin rose higher.

He had to be approaching the first floor of the library.

Kyle squirmed around in the container. He wanted to be all set to roll out the second he was under the reference desk. The Krinkle brothers could be waiting right there. Kyle had to grab the Benjamin Bean box before they did.

His bin reached the top of the wall and flipped forward into another tunnel. This time it was lit. The cardboard carton in front of him disappeared around a curve. Five seconds later, Kyle entered the same turn.

He rumbled six feet down a straightaway.

Some sort of magnetic switch clicked.

The bin tipped sideways to dump its contents.

Kyle tumbled onto the marble floor underneath Ms. Waintraub's desk.

"There he is!" he heard Abia whisper in the distance.

She and Miguel were running to the reference desk from the fiction wall.

Kyle looked around on the floor.

"Where's the Benjamin Bean box?" he asked as quietly as he could.

"They got it!" answered Miguel, keeping his voice hushed. "They had a robo-cart waiting for it the second it popped out of the hole."

"We chased after it," said Abia. "But the robot proved faster than our feet!"

"The bots up here are speedier than the ones downstairs," added Miguel.

"It took the cardboard carton through the bookshelf and into Mr. Lemoncello's office," said Abia. "We must assume that is where the Krinkle brothers are currently situated."

Kyle slumped down onto the floor and kicked off the drone slippers. Miguel tossed him his tennis shoes.

"Where's the shoebox?" Kyle asked as he laced up. "That might be all the proof we actually need. The Benjamin Bean box was a bonus."

Abia looked at Miguel.

Miguel looked at the floor.

"We, uh, sort of lost it," Miguel admitted.

"What?" said Kyle, standing up.

"When we were chasing the robot."

"I thought it was a good and noble idea," said Abia.

"You thought what was a good and noble idea?" asked Kyle.

"To, you know, throw something at the robot," said Miguel.

Kyle's jaw dropped. "You threw Mr. Lemoncello's shoebox at the runaway robot?"

Miguel nodded. "I thought a bop on the head might slow the thing down long enough for Abia to catch it."

"But unfortunately," said Abia, "Miguel threw with far too much force."

"Yeah," said Miguel. "I couldn't believe how hard I hurled that thing, bro. Totally overshot the robot's head and *BOOM!* It landed in the cargo basket. Yo, it was like I threw a perfect Hail Mary touchdown pass in the final seconds to win the game! It was awesome."

"Except we lost the only solid proof we had that Mr. Lemoncello isn't a liar and a thief," Kyle said sadly.

"Yes," said Abia. "That part is not so awesome."

"So," said Kyle, "we failed."

Because, he didn't say out loud, *I tried to take another shortcut and went on Mr. Blue Bin's Wild Ride instead of just using the steps, coming upstairs, and helping Abia and Miguel tackle the runaway robot.*

Kyle put his head in his hands. He was all out of ideas. They'd blown their last shot at clearing Mr. Lemoncello's name.

"You know," said a soft voice behind them, "I failed several times before I was elected president."

It was Abraham Lincoln. Wherever he was, Mr. Raymo had switched on the Nonfictionator.

"When I was young, I went to war a captain and came home a private. I lost my job. I lost eight different elections. I failed in business. Twice."

He gestured toward the other exhibits as they came to animated life and ambled over to where Lincoln was standing.

"In fact," said Lincoln, "that's the one thing we all have in common. Thomas Edison, the Wright brothers, Emily Dickinson, me, even Michael Jordan."

"We were all failures," said Jordan. "I missed more than nine thousand shots in my career. I lost almost three hundred games. Twenty-six times I've been trusted to take the game-winning shot and missed. I've failed over and over and over again in my life. And that is why I succeed."

"Only a dozen of my poems were ever published in my lifetime," said Emily Dickinson.

"My talking doll?" added Edison. "Total disaster!"

"If you've never failed . . . ," said Orville.

". . . you've never tried anything new," his brother, Wilbur, finished.

Kyle grinned.

Abia had been right early on.

There *was* a reason why Mr. Lemoncello chose the historical figures that he did for the new exhibits.

To remind Kyle of what he already knew: No game is ever over until it's over!

51

"That tech wiz Mr. Raymo asked us to give you kids a little pep talk," said the holographic Michael Jordan.

"Dwell in possibility!" declared Emily Dickinson.

"The airplane stays up because it doesn't have the time to fall!" exclaimed Orville Wright.

Miguel scrunched up his face. "Yo. I don't really get that one about the airplane. . . ."

"Many of life's failures," said Thomas Edison, "are people who did not realize how close they were to success when they gave up."

"You're right," said Kyle as a new idea started forming in his head. An idea that might just save Mr. Lemoncello's reputation and the whole library. Maybe by failing with their first idea they could come up with an even better second one!

"Remember how Mr. Raymo instantly whipped up that Lemoncello hologram for the sixth exhibit?" he said.

"Mr. Lemoncello told us he used a three-D camera hidden inside the beak of a ceramic raven in his office," said Abia.

"Exactly," said Kyle. "We just need Mr. Raymo to do it again." He turned to the cluster of famous holograms. "Can you guys, I don't know, summon Mr. Raymo without those two horrible brothers coming out here with him?"

"What do you have against brothers?" asked Orville and Wilbur Wright. They knocked knuckles and did a finger-twiddle pull-away.

"Not you guys. The Krinkles."

"Oh. Okay, then."

Thomas Edison hooked his thumbs into his vest pockets. "Every character generated by the Nonfictionator—a device I would've invented myself, by the way, given sufficient time—sends continuous operational feedback to the motherboard in the core processor. Should there be a malfunction, Mr. Raymo or a member of his staff is immediately summoned to investigate the situation."

"And what qualifies as a malfunction?" asked Kyle.

"A glitch, a hitch, a blip, or a hiccup," said Wilbur Wright.

"For instance," offered Michael Jordan, bouncing his holographic basketball, "if Abe Lincoln started dunking, I'm pretty sure the computer would notice."

"Then let's do it!" said Kyle.

"I hesitate to undertake such an endeavor," said Mr. Lincoln.

"How come?" said Kyle. "You're tall enough to play b-ball!"

"True. But it wouldn't be . . . presidential."

"Look, Abe," said Michael Jordan, "I can accept failure. Everyone fails at something. But I can't accept not trying."

Lincoln stiffened his very long spine. "Very well, then, Air Jordan. Toss me the orange orb and make haste about it. Things may come to those who wait, but only the things left by those who hustle!"

Michael Jordan bounced his ball to Abraham Lincoln.

Lincoln started dribbling it. He even did some flashy moves, rebounding the ball between his long lanky legs.

"Take it to the hoop!" cried Emily Dickinson.

"Fly!" shouted the Wright brothers.

Abraham Lincoln's image spluttered and crackled. His eyeballs started blinking red. But none of that stopped him from running toward the wall, leaping up, soaring skyward, and jamming the basketball over the railing of the second-floor balcony. On the descent, however, his body froze in a leg-splayed leap.

The Lincoln hologram was stuck, sputtering in midair!

Kyle just hoped that was enough of a glitch, hitch, or blip to tear Mr. Raymo away from the Krinkle brothers.

52

Every one of the other holographic characters froze where they stood when the secret panel in the fiction wall swung open.

Kyle, Abia, and Miguel ducked behind the reference desk.

"I'll be right back, gentlemen," they heard Mr. Raymo say. "Slight malfunction in our Abraham Lincoln. We'll want him fully operational for the gala."

"You'd better fix him, Raymo!" shouted the grumpier of the brothers from deep inside Mr. Lemoncello's office. "We need Honest Abe to give us a resounding public endorsement tomorrow night!"

"And then," cried the other brother, "we want Emily Dickinson to play Whoop Dee Doodle Thirteen with all the kids. She's good with words."

"No problem," muttered Mr. Raymo, waiting for the door to the secret passageway to glide shut.

When Kyle was absolutely certain that the Krinkle brothers wouldn't follow Mr. Raymo into the Rotunda Reading Room, he popped up and waved.

"Mr. Keeley!" whispered Mr. Raymo. "Did you create the error code in Abraham Lincoln's software?"

"It was a group effort," Kyle answered modestly. "But, yeah, that was us. We need to ask you a question."

"Please hurry," said Mr. Raymo, looking over his shoulder. "If the brothers catch you kids . . ."

"Mr. Raymo," said Kyle, "can you use your Nonfictionator to replicate anybody saying anything?"

"Yes. But I prefer to have the characters generated by the device speak with historical accuracy. That is why those of us on the Nonfictionator team have put such a high premium on proper research."

"But," said Kyle, "if we did the research and gave you the audio and visual data you needed to create a truthful, honest representation of someone, or *two* someones . . ."

"Then I can easily re-create that person or persons in holographic form," said Mr. Raymo. "It's also extremely helpful if an audio recording exists of the subject. For instance, I am quite confident that we have correctly captured Michael Jordan's authentic voice, since we had primary source material to work with. Abraham Lincoln, on the other hand, sounds like Daniel Day-Lewis from the movie."

"One last thing," Kyle continued. "Can you put these historically accurate characters anywhere in the library? Say, up in the statue nooks?"

"Certainly. Those nooks each have their own holographic projectors, making them one of the easier locations to position a laser-generated character."

"Perfect," said Kyle. "So, um, could you sneak into the control room and fire up your digital recorder? We're about to send you some excellent visuals and audio to work with."

Mr. Raymo looked confused. "I don't fully understand."

"Well, sir, it's like a great American once said: I can accept failure; everyone fails at something. But I can't accept not trying!"

"And what exactly are you *trying* to do?"

"Save Mr. Lemoncello and our library!"

53

Making his way down the secret passageway behind the fiction bookcases to Mr. Lemoncello's office, Kyle thumbed the "3-D Raven-Cam" icon he found on the portable Non-fictionator's universal remote right after "Radio."

Abia and Miguel followed behind him.

"What's our play?" whispered Miguel.

"A little one-on-one interview action," Kyle said in a soft voice. "I hear it's a time-honored investigatory technique."

"Indeed," said Abia.

"What took you so long, Raymo?" snarled one of the Krinkle brothers when they heard the approaching footsteps.

"Sorry," said Kyle when he and his friends stepped into the office. "We're not Mr. Raymo. We're just kids. Beth Bennett sent us."

Kyle could see Mr. Lemoncello's battered shoebox sitting on top of the desk. The Benjamin Bean carton was on the floor—on top of a stack of other cardboard crates, a couple of which were labeled "New Game Ideas."

Next, he checked out the office bookcase. The ceramic raven figurine was sitting on the top shelf. Kyle ambled over to make sure he was standing just below it. Abia and Miguel ambled after him. When the Krinkle brothers spoke, Kyle wanted to make absolutely certain that they were talking directly into the lens of the raven-cam.

"Beth Bennett sent you?" snarled the grumpy brother, Frederick.

"How did you children get into the library?" demanded the other brother, David.

"We learned there is a secret exit reading about Mr. Lemoncello's great library escape game," said Kyle. "And, if you just go backward, it becomes a secret entrance."

"And what, pray tell, are you doing here?" asked David.

"Beth Bennett is my grandmother," said Kyle, without covering his mouth, shuffling his feet, or staring without blinking. "I think you guys know my sister, Jessica, too."

"And we are his besties," said Abia because no way did she or Miguel look like they were related to Kyle.

"Meemaw sent us here," said Kyle.

"Meemaw?" said David Krinkle.

"That's what I call Grandma."

"She would have come herself," said Abia, "but, well, the heat is on, as they say."

"Yeah," added Miguel. "Those guys from TMZ, *Access Hollywood,* and *60 Minutes* are camped out on her front lawn."

"Meemaw wants to make sure you two will be able to keep your end of the deal," said Kyle. "Otherwise, she says, she's blabbing to the press!"

"Now why would Beth Bennett worry about the one hundred thousand dollars we promised to pay her?" sneered David. "She did her job. Everyone believes she is Irma Hirschman. She'll get her money."

"Typical actress," muttered Frederick. "Tell her to go back to playing Mrs. Maplebutter. Oh, wait. She can't. They fired her."

David raised a hand to calm his brother. "Money is not a problem," he told Kyle. "We're very wealthy. Why? Because we know what you kids really want."

"That's right," said Frederick. "For years, we Krinkle brothers have taken the wacky ideas dreamed up by fools like Luigi Lemoncello and made them better."

"And cheaper!" added David.

"You stole ideas from Mr. Lemoncello?" said Kyle. "Impressive."

Now Frederick, his face turning crimson, stepped forward. "We didn't 'steal' ideas from Mr. Lemoncello!" he bellowed. "We improved them."

"Exactly," said David. "When Mr. Lemoncello's disgruntled employee, Benjamin Bean, first came to us in the 1970s with a screwy idea for a picture game coupled with a whoopee cushion, we took that concept and streamlined it. Made it simpler. More accessible to the masses."

"I see," said Kyle. "So this other guy, Benjamin Bean, stole that Whoop Dee Doodle idea from Mr. Lemoncello for you?"

"We didn't 'steal' Whoop Dee Doodle," insisted the furious Frederick. "Benjamin Bean *liberated* Mr. Lemoncello's half-baked, harebrained scheme for us. He brought a poor infant of an idea to a more loving and supportive home."

"For a hefty fee, of course," grumbled David. "We paid him fifty thousand dollars for Mr. Lemoncello's idea."

He checked his watch. "Look, kid, we've got a lot of work to do. . . ."

"What about your new E-Float-E-Cons game?" asked Kyle. "We saw an ad for it on TV. How'd you come up with that cool idea?"

David Krinkle grinned. "Easy. Your big sister, Jessica, found some very interesting blueprints at Mr. Lemoncello's home and sold them to us."

"So go home and tell Miss Jessica Bennett not to worry about her money, either," said Frederick. "She'll be paid as soon as our version of Mr. Lemoncello's floating emoji game rolls off the assembly line. We want to make sure it works before we pay her for *liberating* those blueprints out of the old coot's floor safe."

"Great," said Kyle. "We'll give Jessie the message. Oh,

one last thing. Meemaw wants to know when she's getting her head shot back."

"You mean the publicity still we used to dummy up the game box top?" said David.

"Yeah," said Kyle. "It's her only copy."

"We'll put it in the envelope with her check," said Frederick.

"With the money we make off our version of Mr. Loony-cello's Fantabulous Floating Emoji game," boasted David, "who knows? Maybe they'll both get holiday bonuses!"

The two brothers laughed.

"Yes, sir," said Kyle. "Thank you, sir."

Mr. Raymo entered the office. He was pushing an empty handcart.

"Excuse me," he said. "We need to put those boxes someplace more secure." He gestured toward the shoebox, the Benjamin Bean carton, and the "New Ideas" crates.

"What?" said Frederick. "Why?"

"Mobs of civilians will be traipsing through this building tomorrow night," said Mr. Raymo. "We should keep important documents such as those locked up tight in the control room for the next twenty-four hours. After the gala, we will have more time to properly deal with them."

"I like the way you think, Raymo," said David. "Lock 'em up!"

Mr. Raymo loaded the boxes on his dolly and exited.

Making sure to wink at Kyle on his way out.

"You kids in town through tomorrow?" asked David.

"Yes," said Abia. "We are spending the night at the local Holiday Inn Express."

"Kyle's grandmother is paying for it," said Miguel.

Frederick narrowed his eyes and lowered his suspicious eyebrows. "Who's this Kyle?"

"This other kid we know in Kansas City," said Kyle quickly. "He couldn't make the trip. But his grandmother is friends with my grandmother. She paid for our plane tickets and the motel room. She's our chaperone. She thinks we came here to read."

"Well, see if she'll spring for a second night at the motel," said David. "That way, you kids can come to our grand opening gala tomorrow."

"You bet, sir," said Kyle. "We wouldn't miss it for the world!"

The big event was in less than twenty-four hours.

Kyle just hoped that was enough time for Mr. Raymo to do everything he needed to do to make Kyle's plan work!

54

Of course the library was packed the next night for the Krinkle brothers' big gala.

Kyle's whole family was there. So were all the families of the other local board members. In fact, it felt as if all of Alexandriaville was crowded together under the rotunda—plus TV news crews from the larger Ohio cities. The Chiltingtons and the mayor stood on an elevated platform with Frederick and David Krinkle, all of them smiling for the flashing cameras.

Mr. Raymo wasn't with them.

The chief imagineer was locked behind the red door inside the library's master control room.

So was all the evidence to clear Mr. Lemoncello.

Earlier, Kyle had sent Mr. Raymo the final audio and video files he needed for the *real* show—the stuff Katherine and Elliott scored in Kansas City.

"The food stinks," whined Andrew, nibbling around the edges of a vanilla wafer, the only food the Krinkle brothers served at their party. "The beverages stink, too. The only drink is generic ginger ale."

The Krinkles' new exhibits were the same ones Mr. Lemoncello had planned: Thomas Edison, Michael Jordan, the Wright brothers, Emily Dickinson, and Abraham Lincoln. According to the gala's program, "The Trial of Luigi Lemoncello" would take place later.

David Krinkle presented the new exhibits as if he and his brother had come up with the ideas and created everything themselves.

"As fellow inventors," David announced, "we'd love to hear what Thomas Edison has to say on this grand and auspicious occasion."

The Edison hologram marched across the floor and climbed up the steps to the stage.

"When I single-handedly invented the lightbulb," said the dumbed-down Edison, "I remember thinking, who will pick up my creative spark and carry it forward for the next generation? Thank goodness we have the Krinkle brothers."

The crowd cheered and applauded.

"You guys ready?" Kyle whispered to his friends.

"Go for it, Kyle Keeley," said Abia. "It is definitely time for a shortcut."

Kyle took a deep breath and stepped forward.

"Thomas Edison is right!" he shouted. "The Krinkle

brothers are geniuses. In fact, they deserve to be statues, right here in the library."

On cue, Mr. Raymo, secure in the control room, popped five pairs of Krinkle brother holograms into the ten statue nooks underneath the Wonder Dome.

The audience cheered again.

The Krinkle brothers, onstage, beamed even brighter smiles.

Until their statues started talking.

"We didn't 'steal' Whoop Dee Doodle," said the five Frederick holograms in perfect sync. "Benjamin Bean *liberated* Mr. Lemoncello's half-baked, harebrained scheme for us. He brought a poor infant of an idea to a more loving and supportive home."

"For a hefty fee, of course," grumbled the five statues of David. "We paid him fifty thousand dollars for Mr. Lemoncello's idea."

The audience wasn't cheering so much anymore. In fact, some of them had horrified looks on their faces.

"What goes on here?" said the real David.

"You're that boy from last night!" snarled Frederick. "The grandson!"

Kyle grinned. "Told you I wouldn't miss this gala for anything in the world."

Overhead, the David statues flickered and changed topics.

"Now why would Beth Bennett worry about the one hundred thousand dollars we promised to pay her? She did her job. Everyone believes she is Irma Hirschman. She'll get her money."

"Typical actress," muttered the five Fredericks. "Tell her to go back to playing Mrs. Maplebutter! Tell Miss Jessica Bennett not to worry about her money, either. She'll be paid as soon as our version of Mr. Lemoncello's floating emoji game rolls off the assembly line. We want to make sure it works before we pay her for *liberating* those blueprints out of the old coot's floor safe."

"Enough!" cried the real Frederick. "Mr. Raymo? Turn those fool statues off or you're fired!"

"No can do," replied Mr. Raymo through the sound system. "According to my master schedule, it is now time to play Mr. Lemoncello's Rickety-Trickety Fact or Fictiony game."

"Which," added Kyle, flipping on the wireless microphone Mr. Raymo had rigged him up with, "will show us what happens when you play loosey-goosey with the truthy."

When Kyle said that, a giant lion cage hologram (with an animated lion prowling around inside it) materialized directly above the stage to hover over the Krinkle brothers.

"Okay," said Kyle, doing his best to imitate Mr. Lemoncello's game-show-host voice. "My friends and I have done extensive research and are here today to tell the whole world the truth. Mr. Lemoncello *does* have a patent and a shoebox filled with the stuff that inspired Family Frenzy, including a vintage Barbie doll boot from 1973!"

A hologram of the shoebox, a patent with an embossed seal, and a knee-high go-go boot appeared under the Wonder Dome, which had faded to black to help make the holograms pop.

"Irma Hirschman, on the other hand, never filed for a Family Frolic patent because, well, she never invented a game in her life."

Another hologram appeared: a granny knitting in a rocking chair. It was followed by a Mrs. Maplebutter bottle.

"Because Irma Hirschman, her claims, her website, and everything else about her are fake. She's a character, stolen by the Krinkle brothers, portrayed by an amazing actress, Beth Bennett, who used to be Mrs. Maplebutter and, as you just heard, was paid one hundred thousand dollars to play this new role."

The Wonder Dome became a video screen, filled with a clip of Beth Bennett talking directly into Elliott Schilpp's smartphone lens.

"I'm Beth Bennett. Yes, I am a classically trained actress," she said melodramatically. "But they said I was too old to play Mrs. Maplebutter anymore. Too old? Ha! I am an actress. I defy age! I could play an infant! So when the Krinkle brothers called, I jumped at the chance to play my juiciest role yet! Irma Hirschman—the wronged and weepy game inventor. I already had the costume. I am also available for commercials and corporate appearances." She wiggled her thumb and pinky next to her ear like her hand was a phone. "Call me," she mouthed.

More murmurs of disgust rippled through the audience.

"But wait," said Kyle, "that's not all. Mr. Lemoncello never stole an idea, but the Krinkle brothers sure did. As you've heard the Krinkles confess, Whoop Dee Doodle was Mr. Lemoncello's idea until they paid Benjamin Bean to steal it."

A whoopee cushion appeared overhead.

"And as you've also heard, the Krinkle brothers just stole the blueprints for Mr. Lemoncello's newest creation, the Fantabulous Floating Emoji game."

Akimi leaned in so she could speak into Kyle's lapel mic: "Coming soon to toy stores everywhere."

A hologram of a smiley-face emoji floated between the granny in the rocking chair and the bottle of syrup.

"Put it all together and it's pure Krinkle because it definitely stinkles!"

That was the cue for the Michael Jordan hologram to leap up and slam-dunk a basketball into the whoopee cushion, which set off the teetering Rube Goldberg contraption's chain reaction: The whoopee cushion made a fart sound, expelling a gust of air, which ruffled the patent document. It rolled up like a window shade with a sharp snap that knocked over the shoebox, which made the Barbie boot kick the rail of the rocking chair, which surprised the sweet little old lady so much she flung up her knitting needles, which poked the side of the smiley face's head, which deflated like a balloon and whizzed sideways like a bottle rocket, crashing into the Mrs. Maplebutter bottle, which toppled over and poured a stream of corn syrup goop directly on top of the lion cage, coating the bars with globs of sludge, which made the cage so heavy it slowly drifted down until it trapped both Krinkle brothers underneath it—with the roaring lion.

"Yep," said Kyle, "that's what happens when you keep on lyin'! You end up in the lion cage!"

The crowd laughed and cheered. The TV crews (and every smartphone under the dome) had captured the whole chain reaction. The two police detectives who'd questioned Mr. Lemoncello ambled up onto the stage, probably to ask the Krinkle brothers a few questions, too. The Chiltington family was trying its best to disappear into the walls.

The whole thing was absolutely, incredibly spectacular!

55

Saturday night, there was a second gala at the library.

This one was hosted by Mr. Lemoncello.

The place was, once again, packed.

"Welcome, one and all, to this most wondermous celebration of truth, justice, and the American way!" cried Mr. Lemoncello, who was decked out in a Superman costume for the occasion. Instead of an "S" on his chest, he had a "T" for "truth."

"I'm glad that, thanks to my splendiferous board of trustees, we are all here tonight, laughing at my nightmare!"

The Krinkle brothers had long since fled Alexandria-ville, and they were facing several lawsuits filed by Max Khatchadourian, chief corporate counsel at the Imagination Factory, as well as federal charges of corporate espionage.

The Chiltington family had left Ohio on an extended ski vacation to Switzerland.

The food at Mr. Lemoncello's gala was, of course, out of this world. So were the beverages, including ice-cold Lemonberry Fizz. Balloons were festooned everywhere. Haley Daley flew in from Hollywood and sang her number one hit single "Stop Playin' Games, Baby."

Kyle's whole family was there celebrating with him. His brainiac brother Curtis even got Haley's autograph.

Kyle stood back and beamed, soaking it all in.

After about thirty minutes of laughter, food, music, and video magic from the Wonder Dome, it was finally time to reveal the new holographic attractions.

Thomas Edison told the truth.

Michael Jordan showed off his amazing moves.

Emily Dickinson poetically recited the theme song to *Gilligan's Island* while the Wright brothers swooped around the rotunda with their arms stretched wide.

For the grand finale, Abraham Lincoln finally revealed the fun fact nobody had found in the Fabulous Fact-Finding Frenzy: "I was an animal lover and would neither hunt nor fish."

Seated in a monumental marble chair, he had a cat purring in his lap.

When all the new exhibits were up and running and interacting with the crowds, Kyle and Abia finally gave Mr. Lemoncello the answer to the last question in the Fabulous Fact-Finding Frenzy.

"The inspiration for your game Family Frenzy was your big crazy family," said Kyle.

"Your nine brothers and sisters: Alberto, Arianna, Fabio, Francesca, Lucrezia, Mary, Massimo, Sofia, and Tomasso," said Abia.

"Your mother and father, Angelica and Angelo. Your dog, Fusilli, and your cat, Stromboli," added Kyle.

"Congratulicitations, Kyle and Abia! You are the first team to give me the correct answer. Therefore, you officially win the Fabulous Fact-Finding Frenzy. You will be going on tour with the new exhibits and receive . . ."

Mr. Lemoncello pulled back a black velvet cloth to reveal two shiny, shrink-wrapped game boxes.

". . . the first copies, hot off the presses, of my brand-new Fantabulous Floating Emoji game!"

Kyle's eyes nearly popped out of his skull.

His mouth hung open. A little drool might've dribbled out, too.

And he couldn't believe he was about to say what he was about to say.

"Thanks," he squeaked. "But, uh, we'd officially like to give all of our prizes to Akimi and Angus."

Mr. Lemoncello looked flabbergasted. "My gast has been flabbered. Why would you two give away your prizes?"

"We promised we would," said Abia, because Kyle was too busy staring sadly at the two shiny game boxes.

"That's okay," said Angus, stepping forward. "You guys can keep the games."

"Yeah," said Akimi. "Kyle would just come over to my house and beat me at it anyway."

"Plus," said Angus, "I liked how you stuck it to those Krinkle brothers last night. You saved the library, dude."

"Not by myself," said Kyle. "I had a ton of help. Everyone played a part."

"Very well, then." Mr. Lemoncello turned to face the crowd. "Dr. Zinchenko?"

"She's back?" asked Kyle.

"Oh, yes," said Mr. Lemoncello. "Arrived early this morning after changing planes in New York City, where she dropped by the Imagination Factory to pick up a few gift items for me."

Dr. Zinchenko—who was very hard to miss with her red dress, red heels, red eyeglasses, and red hair—wheeled a library cart across the rotunda floor.

It was loaded down with ten more copies of Fantabulous Floating Emoji!

"Everybody gets a game!" announced Mr. Lemoncello. Then he started pointing at all the trustees in the crowd. "You get a game, and you get a game, and you get a game!"

"Woo-hoo!" shouted Miguel.

"But wait!" declared Mr. Lemoncello. "There's more. Time for another surprise: Instead of just one team going on a whirlwind tour, all twelve of you will travel to libraries across North America with our new exhibits."

"Yes!" said Andrew Peckleman. "I've always wanted to visit Vancouver!"

"And that's not all," said Mr. Lemoncello. "In gratitude for all that you twelve trustees have done in your unrelenting quest for the truth and your refusal to accept the first answer as the only answer, I hereby decree that a new set of statues fill the nooks of the Rotunda Reading Room for the coming week! Mr. Raymo, if you please?"

One by one, five of the ten alcoves were illuminated with new holographic images: pairs of statues featuring the teams of the Fabulous Fact-Finding Frenzy: Elliott Schilpp and Katherine Kelly, Miguel Fernandez and Pranav Pillai, Sierra Russell and Jamal Davis, Andrew Peckleman and Diane Capriola, Akimi Hughes and Angus Harper.

"What about Kyle and Abia?" asked Akimi.

"Well," said Mr. Lemoncello, "I knew those two would never be able to find a way to work together, to truly become a team, to forget what they thought they knew about each other and find out the truth. So we're giving them each their own separate nooks."

A holographic Kyle popped up on the opposite side of the rotunda from the holographic Abia.

"Mr. Lemoncello?" said Kyle. "You're wrong. We made a fantastic team."

Mr. Lemoncello arched an eyebrow. "Is that a fact? Can you prove it?"

Abia grinned. "Definitely, sir. It's true."

"Well then, Abia, I'm glad I did this one-on-one interview with you."

"It is a time-honored investigatory technique, sir," said Kyle.

"Indeed so! Mr. Raymo, if you please?"

Lights flickered.

The Kyle hologram faded away and then popped up in the nook alongside Abia.

"Congratulations, Kyle," said Abia, extending her hand.

Kyle took it . . . but paused midshake.

"Wait a second. That's the first time you didn't use my last name. You didn't call me Kyle Keeley."

"I know," Abia said with a smile. "Because now we are more than teammates. We are friends."

The party continued. Haley Daley sang her other big hit, "Game On, Baby!"

Some kids danced.

So did Mad Dog, the bookmobile driver, and Dr. Zinchenko.

Together.

Sierra Russell and Jamal Davis sat down to read their books. Elliott Schilpp ate six chili dogs. Michael Jordan taught Kyle's brother Michael how to dribble a ball between his legs.

After the song ended, Kyle made his way over to the center desk, where Dr. Zinchenko was cutting a huge sheet cake with "Congratulicitations" scrolled across it in bright red frosting.

"Can I ask you a question?" he asked her.

"Of course."

"Did your mother really make a birthday wish about turning Mr. Lemoncello into a hologram?"

"Maybe. Maybe not."

The holographic librarian, Ms. Waintraub, appeared beside Dr. Zinchenko. "I'm afraid you would need to do extensive research to find out the truth," she said.

"And if you did," said Dr. Zinchenko, "you might discover that this holographic reference librarian identified a threat to the library when the Krinkle brothers unexpectedly turned up here in Ohio."

"I did," said Ms. Waintraub.

"You might also learn," said Dr. Zinchenko, "that her software is programmed to automatically transmit perceived dangers directly to me, no matter where in the world I might be located. Furthermore, if, in your research, you were to interview me, Dr. Yanina Zinchenko, you might realize that if I could not be present to protect Mr. Lemoncello in a time of crisis, then there is only one other individual whom I would trust to do that job for me. Someone I needed to be in the library this week. Someone who would do whatever it took to defend Mr. Lemoncello."

Kyle gulped a little. "Me?"

Dr. Zinchenko grinned. "Ah. Very good, Mr. Keeley. In this instance, your first answer *is* the correct answer. And may I add one more thing?"

"Sure."

"Thank you for doing my job so well."

IS THE RACE OVER?

Of course not!

There is one more puzzle in the book that wasn't in the story, although there were several clues about how to find it. (And, yes, it could be that simple.) So do your research and send your answer to author@ChrisGrabenstein.com.

AUTHOR'S NOTE

Flop. Failure. Fiasco.

Not words you usually associate with Abraham Lincoln, Emily Dickinson, Thomas Edison, the Wright brothers, and Michael Jordan.

Well, how about J. K. Rowling, Albert Einstein, Oprah Winfrey, Walt Disney, Lucille Ball, the Beatles, Steve Jobs, Charlie Chaplin, and Dr. Seuss? All these famously successful people failed before they succeeded.

They had to dust themselves off, pick themselves up, and try again.

Robert Kennedy once said, "Only those who dare to fail greatly can ever achieve greatly."

Or as Thomas Edison put it, "Many of life's failures are experienced by people who did not realize how close they were to success when they gave up."

Resilience is what attracted me to the historical figures selected for the new displays in Mr. Lemoncello's Library—the ability to spring back into shape after being bent, stretched, or rejected.

We sometimes forget how much hard work went into what now seems so obvious. Dr. Seuss was my favorite author when I was a kid. I just took for granted that his genius was destined to be recognized, that his books were bound to be published. I never realized that Theodor Seuss Geisel's first book, *And to Think That I Saw It on Mulberry Street,* was rejected by twenty-seven different publishers. Legend has it he was on his way home to burn the manuscript when he bumped into a college classmate who had just that very morning started a job as a children's book editor.

Oh, the places we readers never would've gone if Dr. Seuss had given up on Mulberry Street.

My first bestseller, *Escape from Mr. Lemoncello's Library,* was almost never published. I worked on it for two years and rewrote 50 percent of the manuscript eight different times. My editor and I almost gave up and said, "Let's burn the manuscript and write something else."

I'm so glad we didn't.

I'm also glad that while working on that book I had Chinese food for dinner one night. Inside my fortune cookie was a slip of paper with these words of wisdom: "Fall down seven times, stand up eighth time."

I taped that fortune to my computer monitor and kept clacking on the keyboard.

It's like the famous football coach Vince Lombardi said: "It's not whether you get knocked down, it's whether you get up."

MR. LEMONCELLO'S GREAT LIBRARY RACE BOOK LIST

Here's a complete list of the books mentioned or alluded to in *Mr. Lemoncello's Great Library Race.* How many have *you* read?

- ☐ *The Age of Edison: Electric Light and the Invention of Modern America* by Ernest Freeberg
- ☐ *Alexander and the Terrible, Horrible, No Good, Very Bad Day* by Judith Viorst
- ☐ *Charlie and the Chocolate Factory* by Roald Dahl
- ☐ *Cloudy with a Chance of Meatballs* by Judi Barrett and Ron Barrett
- ☐ *The Crossover* by Kwame Alexander
- ☐ *The Ear, the Eye, and the Arm* by Nancy Farmer
- ☐ The Encyclopedia Brown series by Donald J. Sobol
- ☐ *Escape from Mr. Lemoncello's Library* by Chris Grabenstein
- ☐ *Everything on a Waffle* by Polly Horvath
- ☐ *Finding the Worm* by Mark Goldblatt
- ☐ *Fortunately, the Milk* by Neil Gaiman
- ☐ *Frindle* by Andrew Clements
- ☐ *The Gollywhopper Games* by Jody Feldman
- ☐ The Harry Potter series by J. K. Rowling

- ☐ *Hatchet* by Gary Paulsen
- ☐ *The Higher Power of Lucky* by Susan Patron
- ☐ *Horton Hatches the Egg* by Dr. Seuss
- ☐ *Julie of the Wolves* by Jean Craighead George
- ☐ *Laughing at My Nightmare* by Shane Burcaw
- ☐ *Lawrence of Arabia: The Authorized Biography of T. E. Lawrence* by Jeremy Wilson
- ☐ *The Lion, the Witch and the Wardrobe* by C. S. Lewis
- ☐ *Mike Mulligan and His Steam Shovel* by Virginia Lee Burton
- ☐ *Oh, the Places You'll Go!* by Dr. Seuss
- ☐ *Penny from Heaven* by Jennifer L. Holm
- ☐ The Percy Jackson and the Olympians series by Rick Riordan
- ☐ *Peter Pan* by J. M. Barrie
- ☐ *Pinocchio* by Carlo Collodi
- ☐ *The Puzzling World of Winston Breen* by Eric Berlin
- ☐ *Roget and His Thesaurus* by Jen Bryant
- ☐ *Seabiscuit: An American Legend* by Laura Hillenbrand
- ☐ *Timmy Failure: Mistakes Were Made* by Stephan Pastis
- ☐ *Unstoppable* by Tim Green
- ☐ *The Very Hungry Caterpillar* by Eric Carle
- ☐ *The Westing Game* by Ellen Raskin
- ☐ *Wicked: The Life and Times of the Wicked Witch of the West* by Gregory Maguire
- ☐ *Wonder* by R. J. Palacio
- ☐ *The Wonderful Wizard of Oz* by L. Frank Baum
- ☐ *A Year Down Yonder* by Richard Peck

THANK YOU . . .

No Lemoncello book would be possible without the help of a bazillion wondermous people:

My wife and first editor (not to mention the love of my life), J.J.

The librarian whose school I visited and whose name I wish I could remember, because she's the one who told me I should do a book about research meaning re-searching.

My Random House editor, Shana Corey, who is so much fun to work with. You should read her book *The Secret Subway*, about New York's first subway. She knows how to make research fun!

Special thanks to editorial assistant Maya Motayne, who, in addition to everything else, tallies up all the books mentioned in these books!

My agent, Eric Myers, and the whole team at Dystel, Goderich and Bourret.

Copyeditors and book dedicatees Barbara Bakowski and Alison Kolani. I hope I spelled their names correctly.

Art director Nicole de las Heras and cover artist extraordinaire Gilbert Ford.

Production manager Tim Terhune (because these books are quite a production).

Special thanks to all of Mr. Lemoncello's friends at Random House Children's Books who have done so much to get his books into the hands of so many kiddos: John Adamo, Kerri Benvenuto, Judith Haut, Jules Kelly, Kim Lauber, Mallory Loehr, Barbara Marcus, Michelle Nagler, and Stephanie O'Cain.

Dr. Zinchenko would like to personally thank Mr. Lemoncello's special friends in the RHCB School and Library Marketing department: Laura Antonacci, Lisa Nadel, Kristin Schulz, and the very real (and not at all robotic) Adrienne Waintraub.

Public thanks to all Mr. Lemoncello's extra-special friends in the publicity department: Dominique Cimina, Aisha Cloud, Cassie McGinty, and Casey Ward.

And where would the Imagination Factory be without the sensational sales team led by Felicia Frazier? Thanks to Joe English, Bobbie Ford, Becky Green, Kimberly Langus, Deanna Meyeroff, Sarah Nasif, Mark Santella, Richard Vallejo, and the entire Random House sales team, who were, and still are, some of Mr. Lemoncello's most ardent supporters.

Finally, thanks to all the parents, teachers, librarians, kids, and readers who send me emails, drawings of your favorite characters, and sweet thank-you cards. You guys make me smile every day.

BONUS CLUE

Want to solve the extra puzzle mentioned before the author's note? The one that was "in the book" but not "in the story"? Here's a HUGE hint . . . if you can figure out the answer to one more rebus!

BOYS AND GIRLS, READERS AND GAMERS OF ALL AGES—ARE YOU READY TO PLAY

MR. LEMONCELLO'S

BIGGEST, MOST DAZZLING GAME YET?!

After months of anticipation, Mr. Lemoncello is taking his games LIVE on the world-famous Kidzapalooza Television Network! Everyone's invited to audition, but only a lucky few will be chosen to compete in front of millions of viewers for the biggest prize of all.

Kyle Keeley is determined that he'll be one of the final competitors. Each of the winning teams will have to make it through the twists and turns of five separate rooms, cracking the codes and solving the puzzles that unlock each room and allow the kids to BREAK OUT. But nothing is ever as it seems with Mr. Lemoncello, and the surprises in store just might stump even the game master himself!

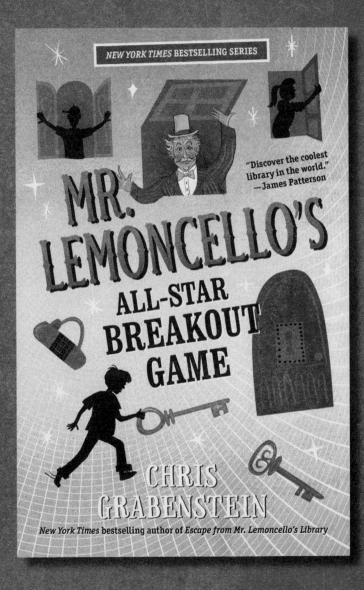

"Discover the coolest
library in the world."
—James Patterson

MR. LEMONCELLO'S

ALL-STAR BREAKOUT GAME

CHRIS GRABENSTEIN

New York Times bestselling author of *Escape from Mr. Lemoncello's Library*

Coming in 2019!

Ready for some OUTRAGEOUS fun in the sun?

Take a vacation in a book with Chris Grabenstein's Welcome to Wonderland series!

"Nonstop hilarity—five stars!" —Lincoln Peirce, Big Nate series

"So funny I fell off the bed!" —Izzy B., age 10

Winner of the Sid Fleischman Humor Award

TURN THE PAGE TO START READING BOOK ONE.

Gator Tales

Like I told my friends at school, living in a motel is always exciting—especially during an alligator attack.

"To this day, nobody knows how that giant alligator made it up to the second-floor balcony of my family's motel on St. Pete Beach," I told my audience.

The cafeteria was so quiet you could've heard a taco shell snap.

"Maybe it took the steps. Maybe it just stood up, locked its teeth on a porch railing, and flipped itself up and over in a mighty somersault swoop. The thing was strong, people. Very, very strong.

"I heard Clara, my favorite housekeeper, scream, '¡Monstruo, Señor Wilkie! ¡Monstruo!'

"'Run!' I shouted, because Clara's always been like a second mom to me and I wanted her to be alive enough to see her daughter graduate from med school.

"Well, she didn't need me to shout it twice. Clara abandoned her laundry cart while that alligator raced toward the room at the far end of the balcony. And I knew why: the chicken.

"See, the family in room 233—a mom, a dad, two kids, and a baby—had just gone upstairs with a whole bucket of the stuff. Heck, I could smell it twenty doors down. The giant alligator? He smelled that secret blend of eleven herbs and spices all the way back at his little lake on the Bayside Golf Course, where, legend has it, he's chomped off a few ball divers' arms.

"Thinking fast and running faster, I made it to Clara's deserted laundry cart. I grabbed a few rolls of toilet paper and lobbed them like hand grenades. The T.P. conked the gator on his head just as he was about to chomp through the terrified family's door.

"That's when the giant lizard whipped around.

He looked at me with those big bowling-ball eyes. Forget the chicken. He wanted *me*! He roared like smelly thunder and sprinted down the balcony.

"I just grinned. Because the gator was doing exactly what I wanted him to do. While he barreled ahead on stubby legs, I braced my feet on the bumper of the laundry cart. I lashed several towels together to create a long terry-cloth lasso. I twirled it over my head. I waited for my moment.

"When the gator was five, maybe six, feet away, I flung out my towel rope, aiming for his wide-open mouth. He clamped down. I tugged back. My lasso locked on a jagged tooth. 'Hee-yah!' I shouted. 'Giddyup!' The monster took off.

"What happened next, you wonder? Well, I rode that laundry cart all the way back to the crazy alligator's golf course, where I sent the gator scurrying down into its water hazard. 'And stay away from our motel,' I hollered, and I guess that gator listened, because he's never dared return."

When I finished, everyone applauded, even Ms. Nagler, the teacher on cafeteria duty. She raised her hand to ask a question.

"Yes, ma'am?"

"How'd you and the alligator get down from the second floor?"

I winked. "One step at a time, Ms. Nagler. One step at a time."

She, and everybody else, laughed.

Yep, everybody at Ponce de León Middle School loves a good P. T. Wilkie story.

Except, of course, Mr. Frumpkes.

He came into the cafeteria just in time to hear my big finish.

And like always, he wasn't smiling.

Truth and Consequences

"**M**r. Wilkie?" Mr. Frumpkes had his hands on his hips and his eyes on me. "Lunch is over."

Right on cue, the bell signaling the end of lunch period started clanging.

Fact: Alligators cannot run fast for long distances. They are cold-blooded and therefore quickly deplete their energy reserves. The alligator in your story could NOT have transported you to a golf course two miles away.

Between you and me, I sometimes think Mr. Frumpkes has telepathic powers. He can make the class-change bell ring just by thinking about it.

"Ah," he said, clearly enjoying the earsplitting rattle and clanks. "Now we don't have to listen to any more of Mr. Wilkie's outrageously ridiculous tales!"

My first class right after lunch?

History with Mr. Frumpkes, of course.

He paced back and forth at the front of the room with his hands clasped behind his back.

"Facts are important, boys and girls," he said. "They lead us to the truth. Here at the Ponce de León Middle School, we have a motto: 'Vincit omnia veritas!'"

I couldn't resist making a wisecrack. "I thought our school motto was 'Go, Conquistadors!'"

Mr. Frumpkes stopped pacing so he could glare at me some more.

"'Vincit omnia veritas' is Latin, Mr. Wilkie. It means 'The truth conquers all.'"

"So it is like 'Go, Conquistadors!' because conquistadors conquered stuff and—"

"I'm beginning to understand why your father never shows up at parent-teacher conferences, Mr. Wilkie."

Okay. That hurt. My ears were burning.

"But since Mr. Wilkie seems fixated on con-

·quistadors," said Mr. Frumpkes, "here is everybody's brand-new homework assignment."

"Awww," groaned the whole classroom.

"Don't groan at me. Groan at your immature classmate! Thanks to Mr. Wilkie, you are all required to write a one-thousand-word essay filled with cold, hard facts about the man whom this middle school is named after: the famous Spanish conquistador Ponce de León. Your papers are due on Monday."

"Whoa," said my friend Pinky Nelligan. "Monday is the start of Spring Break."

"Fine," said Mr. Frumpkes. "Your papers are due tomorrow. Friday."

More groans.

"Let this be a lesson to you all: facts are more important than fiction."

I was about to disagree and tell Mr. Frumpkes that I think some stories have more power than all the facts you can find on Google.

But I didn't.

Because *everybody* in the classroom was making stink faces at me.

I Scream, You Scream

I refused to let Mr. Frumpkes win.

"Oh, before I forget—quick announcement: you guys are all invited to the Wonderland Motel after school today. My grandpa wants to try out his new outdoor ice-cream dispenser. The ice cream is free, limit one per guest."

The groans and moans of my classmates turned into whoops of joy. Mr. Frumpkes tried to restore order by banging on his desk with a tape dispenser.

"We're here to discuss history, Mr. Wilkie! Not free ice cream!"

But everybody loves free ice cream.

That's just a cold, hard fact.

Unless it's soft-serve.

Then it's kind of custardy.

Welcome to Wonderland

The Wonderland, the motel my family owns and operates on St. Pete Beach, used to be called Walt Wilkie's Wonder World.

It was a resort and small-time amusement park my grandfather opened back in October 1970—exactly one year before that other Walt opened Disney World over in Orlando.

"We had a very good year, P.T.," Grandpa always tells me. "A very good year."

Now the Wonderland is just a motel with a lot of wacky decorations and tons of incredible stories but not too many paying customers.

There's even a sausage-and-cheese-loving mouse out back named Morty D. Mouse. Grandpa was going to call him Mikey Mouse, but, well, like I said, Disney World opened.

My mom is the motel manager. I think that's why she frowns a lot and nibbles so many pencils. The Wonderland can "barely make ends meet," she tells me. Constantly. That means we'll never be rich hotel tycoons like the Hiltons, I guess.

Mom and I live in room 101/102, right behind the front desk. The lobby is our living room (complete with two soda machines, a snack pantry, and tons of brochures).

Grandpa lives in a one-bedroom apartment over the maintenance shed near the swimming pool.

He likes to tinker with his "attractions" back there. Right now, he is trying to fix up a smiling goober he bought from a "Hot Boiled Peanuts" stand in Georgia. He thinks with enough green, orange, and yellow paint, he can turn Mr. Peanut into some sort of smiling tropical fruit—like that's all the Wonderland needs to make it *Florida Fun in the Sun* magazine's "Hottest Family Attraction in the Sunshine State" (a title Grandpa really wants to snatch away from Disney World someday).